FLYING AGAINST THE WIND

G.D.K. Huffman

Library of Congress Control Number: 2025914721

ISBN 978-1-963222-05-0 (paperback) | ISBN 978-1-963222-06-7 (hardback) | ISBN 978-1-963222-04-3 (ebook)

To all the people who supported me even when I chose to fly against the wind.

Thank you for saving me from the Gaité.

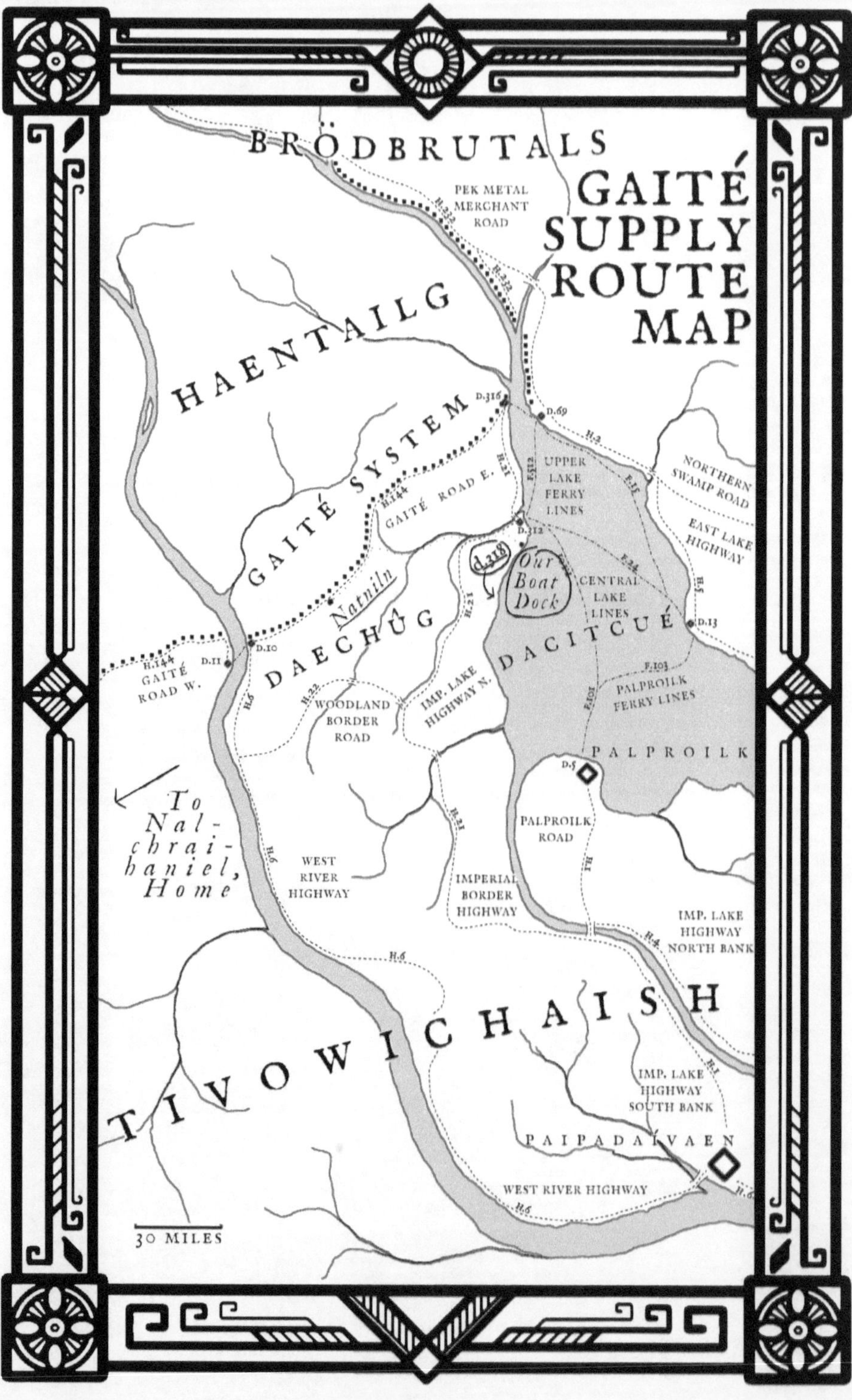

BRÖDBRUTALS
GAITÉ SUPPLY ROUTE MAP
HAENTAILG
PEK METAL MERCHANT ROAD
H.332
H.332
GAITÉ SYSTEM
D.316
D.69
H.2
Natniln
H.144
GAITÉ ROAD E.
H.31
F.512
UPPER LAKE FERRY LINES
NORTHERN SWAMP ROAD
F.31
EAST LAKE HIGHWAY
D.312
DAECHÚG
D.318
Our Boat Dock
CENTRAL LAKE LINES
F.24
B.5
D.13
H.144
D.11
D.10
H.21
DACITCUÉ
F.103
GAITÉ ROAD W.
H.6
H.22
WOODLAND BORDER ROAD
IMP. LAKE HIGHWAY N.
F.101
PALPROILK FERRY LINES
To Nal-chrai-haniel, Home
H.21
PALPROILK
D.5
PALPROILK ROAD
H.9
WEST RIVER HIGHWAY
H.1
IMPERIAL BORDER HIGHWAY
IMP. LAKE HIGHWAY NORTH BANK
H.4
H.6
TIVOWICHAISH
H.1
IMP. LAKE HIGHWAY SOUTH BANK
PAIPADAIVAEN
30 MILES
WEST RIVER HIGHWAY
H.6
H.6

Contents

1 The Kite

Lapiutalnice stared off just past the spinning windmill, out into the deep blue of the sky beyond. It was brilliant that afternoon, the puffy clouds billowing up from the southern seas blurring the blue canvas with strokes of white and gray, occasionally providing shade from the sun as she drifted across the heavens. At the center of it all was what held his attention, however: a single point of vibrant color, standing in stark contrast to the blues and whites around it. The child's red kite rode the same breeze that powered the spinning sails it was almost hidden by, bouncing and swaying as if on a rolling sea.

How long he had been sitting there enraptured by the sleek gliding toy? The elf man did not know, nor did he care. Nestled in a bale of hay just in front of the barn, he would have been content to watch that kite there forever. It was a truly beautiful day, and it had been a long time since he had been able to enjoy one like he had as a kid, flying his own kite along the shores of the Nalchraihaniel, watching the great sails of the merchant ships pass by his small coastal hometown. These days he only flew kites for research, when he had the chance, and had not seen a galleon for the better part of a decade.

For there were no great ships along the dusty roads of Natniln or anywhere in Daechûg, for that matter, except the smaller vessels which sailed the lake. Lapiutalnice's wife tried to get him there often, she said to get him to shut up about boats, but that couldn't be the real reason. She was very smart and knew very well that those trips only encouraged his "extravagant hobby," as she called it. Sadly, the Gaité at which the Fienlapus were posted was a three-day horse ride from Dacitcué –and thus a small commitment to go out that way.

Today he contented himself in watching the kite instead of flying one, cherishing every moment that he was off duty. He probably should have been catching up on more of his farm duties, but the injury he had suffered while training made that difficult. Not that he was complaining – Lapiutalnice's leave from the army was very opportune. It finally gave him time to focus on his project which he did not normally have, despite his work at the fort being comprised of staring out over the steppe for hours on end with little to do.

Unfortunately, the empress in Paipadaívaen did think it was important to watch the sea of grass. Thus, by mandate of the City of a Thousand Trees, he had few free moments to do what he wished to be doing that very moment if not enjoying the clouds drifting by. With that reminder of the task at hand, he glanced toward the dirt path leading out of the farm. Beyond, he could see the scattered fields and houses of Natniln, but no horse and cart yet. Nulaidutice was running late this afternoon, it was probably taking her awhile to find the steel rods he had requested. They were normally sold directly to the Gaité for use in gun repair, but he couldn't see why the excess wouldn't be sold to normal citizenry.

He hoped so at least – he needed them to continue. Craning his neck to look back into the barn, he sighed. The inside space was mostly taken up by a large object covered in canvas, sitting there idly until his wife got off her own work. A cat sat nestled on top for the time being, enjoying the snug warm shade of the barn while it wasn't filled with the sound of beating metal or sawing timber. A rare event since Lapiutalnice's injury. Another feline could be seen yawning atop the bundles of canvas and lumber which were stacked nearby, waiting to be used. Everything was still in order; all that needed to be done was wait.

Turning back to the sky, Lapiutalnice settled in to do just that.

It turned out to be awhile longer, and with the warm sun peeking out between the clouds, the elf man must have fallen asleep. For he didn't remember ever hearing the cart approach, nor the horse being unharnessed, nor the approach of the cross-looking elf woman whose face now blocked the patch of sky where the kite had once been. "Oh there you are, Nulai," he smiled, totally unconcerned with the glare he was receiving. "Did you have a nice day out in town?"

"You lazy oaf," she was trying to say sternly, but his confidence already was cracking her façade. "You've been lying here the entire time I was gone, haven't you?" Though trying to look menacing, being built like a twig wasn't helping her case. Granted, Lapiutalnice was not all that much larger, but his military training had given him a bit of an edge. At least he was somewhat muscular for an elf, and probably would have considered himself strong if he had never met orc scouting parties while he was out on patrol. After seeing one of those gray-skinned goliaths no elf intimidated him anymore. And he tried to stay as far away from patrol as he possibly could.

"Did you find any rods out and about?" he continued without answering the question. "I hope so or I might have to try and pester the captain for some. And we both know what he thinks about me." He added the last part with a chuckle, though he meant it too. He didn't exactly impress his overseer, and his lack of care for the captain's opinion would have frustrated the man greatly. But the comment did manage to soften his wife's face a bit. She tried to maintain the scowl but failed to keep it up in the eyes any longer.

"It's your lucky day," she sighed, waving toward the barn. "I already put them next to your mad scheme, which frankly made them very hard to buy. They know all these supplies I'm buying are going to something strange, and it's not a good look, mister. Not exactly much use for someone like me to be buying a bunch of steel rods, is there?"

"Well," Lapiutalnice said, sitting up, "I did offer to buy them myself, dear, and save you the trouble." He tried to stand, but Nulaidutice was not about to have it. Before he could protest, she had her arm around him and was guiding him to his feet. He was pretty sure it was unnecessary, but she wasn't going to let him find out and hurt himself falling like last week.

"It's still my money, stupid," she snapped, leading him into the barn where she knew he wanted to go. "You think the military is paying you anything while you're away from the Gaité? You're lucky you've beguiled some woman enough to pull you out while injured to heal instead of sweeping the fort until you can shoot a gun again." Setting him down between the canvas-covered object and the supplies she had brought in, she quickly moved to the back of the barn. There she started loading up a box with various tools, occasionally holding one up to confirm that her husband would need it.

"I don't know what I did to appease Lady Luck so either, but you aren't going to find me complaining," he replied warmly, "At least if I were out and about doing it, there is a less likely chance that they'd attach your face to it, and maybe you'd be spared a little bit."

To this she grunted, the amusement having left her eyes a bit, though that was partially due to her lugging over the huge toolbox she had just assembled. "Doubt it would help much, ladies gossip Lapiu, and they aren't going to leave me out of the fun. It isn't that bad though, the Plains Elves just assume it is some new High Elf fad I picked up in university. Pampering your husbands or something like that. They come to some weird conclusions out here." This might have been true, but Lapiutalnice also knew it was just as likely that it was her hair color as much as her university degree that was sparing her the brunt of it. A wall of superficial concerns that would not hold forever.

Her ruffled blonde hair was the mark of a High Elf lineage, a sign to the border elves that she came from the heart of the empire. It was only logical to put up with some of her antics, as she likely had connections in Tivowichaisch, connections it would be better to be on the good side of. Yet beyond this superficiality, another mark of her heritage could be seen faintly on her face: the freckles that outed her Wood Elf relations, and similar origins at the edge of the imperial heartland. In university she'd had to fight to be accepted by her peers from powerful political families, but out here at the edge of the steppe no one knew that. In Daechûg anyone with blonde hair was assumed to have some stature because the only ones they ever met were officials and engineers from the silver forest. Even Sea Elf soldiers were rarely relocated into the area – Lapiutalnice was just one of the unlucky few because he had some Plains Elf relatives who might take him if he ever became unfit for service on the bloody orc frontier.

"Well, I don't mind this new fad," he chuckled once again, taking a pair of tongs and hammer from the box as his wife moved to uncover the object of his labors. "And I'm sure I'm not the only soldier out there who wouldn't mind their wife taking an interest in their projects."

"Don't wrap me up in this," Nulaidutice retorted, despite now moving over to light the compact forge for her husband's use. "It's not my fault you're the only man in the whole empire with a dream to accomplish something. I just have to keep you busy so you don't tear the house apart to realize your mad vision."

"It's more of a shed really," her husband replied with a smirk, "not at all like the elegant stone buildings on the coast or the treetop cities in the woods. The Plains Elves are nice enough and all, but their houses feel just like the barns they pride themselves on. It really wouldn't be any loss."

"Hey!" Her reply came accompanied by a loose coal being thrown at him. "I design those barns you know, and I didn't spend two decades in university to have my husband mock them."

"It really is a loss on their part," Lapiutalnice laughed, reaching into the tool-box to remove the wrenches he wanted, then began inspecting boxes of bolts, "If they had kept you designing wagons instead of their timber cubes we probably wouldn't have to worry about drought season anymore."

"Dear, you are a soldier, you know the Gaités are important for keeping the orcs out of our lands," his wife sighed, pushing over the super-heated furnace to the waiting project.

"Bah, I've only seen orc clans a few times, and never have they engaged us. All of them far from the Gaités. They aren't imbeciles, they learned generations back that charging into a musket line isn't ideal for their health. We could have stopped building Gaités a century ago and still be safe," he chuckled to himself, knowing full well that Nulaidutice had heard his argument a million times before. Reaching forward, he grasped at the side of canvas and gave it a hardy tug.

His effort was met by a snort from his wife, and a snarky comment, but after she pitched in her efforts, as well, they uncovered the wooden frame underneath. "It still doesn't look like a boat," was all she said after taking the progress in for a few seconds, causing Lapiutalnice to grin and roll his eyes.

"Well what do you want to call her then?" he retorted as he began to beat one of the steel rods into a hook. "It carries passengers through the sky like a boat does over water. A Lapudrum is very fitting in that case, at least in my opinion."

"The wings make it look more like a bird," Nulaidutice pointed toward the naked wooden ribs that would eventually be covered in tense canvas. "And don't play coy, I saw you taking measurements of the pigeon's wings a week ago, right before you made them."

"Piqoug wasn't around, so I had to make do. And me asking you to help calculate the amount of lift the shape would create before doing so didn't give me away?" Lapiutalnice couldn't help but laugh. "But unlike a pigeon she won't rely on flapping her wings to stay airborne."

"That's good," she interjected, pointing toward the central body which, to be fair, looked much more like a boat. "Because you literally nailed the wings into the frame. You'd be restarting if you wanted it to flap, and I'm not sure either of us could handle that."

"I couldn't think of a good mechanism to hold onto the wings that could both flap and be sturdy. Besides, at its weight Piqoug says that flapping wouldn't help much. He actually suggested I use the principle of soaring, where the lift from the Lapudrum moving will be what keeps her airborne," he smirked, proud of knowing such technical terms despite his schooling barely teaching him how to read. "Sort of like a hawk or buzzard, or even a kite, but she'd have to be going much faster since she weighs so much."

The elf woman sighed, raising her eyebrows in his direction as he began to sift through the bucket of bolts to fit his steel strut in place. Placing her hands on her hips, she said, "And how are you planning on getting your sky boat to go that fast, dear?"

"Well, you see, I was thinking we could put a thing on the front, like the windmill inverted. As it spins it will carry the machine forward. From the math I tricked you into doing for me, I found out if it was spinning fast enough it could drag the Lapudrum forward fast enough for lift to kick in and keep her airborne," he said proudly, though his brilliance was met with a mock cuff to the back of his head.

"Doofus, so the windmill wasn't damaged!" She was trying so hard to act annoyed at being tricked into spending a whole afternoon fixing it but was clearly on the verge of laughing at this point.

"I would never lie to you, dear," he winked while rubbing the back of his head, feigning injury. "Though I may or may not have engineered its failure and greatly exaggerated the damage."

"Well, alright, you win this time, stupid," she said, turning her head to hide the wide grin that was forming, "But what under the sun do you think can get this device of yours spinning fast enough?"

"That... I have no answer for right now unfortunately," he said and began to zone out for a moment, thinking on the issue. The major roadblock between him and actually building a flying machine. His wife's math checked out, the aerodynamics should be sound, but if it could not go fast enough it would never fly. He would have dwelt on this issue for much longer if it wasn't for the squeezing of his shoulders snapping him out of it. "For now, I just plan to take it sailing on the lake and let the boat generate the energy needed, like a kid running with a kite. I'm hoping to have it ready for that in a week when you said we'd go again."

With that said, he grabbed one of the twig-like hands, and looking back at his wife standing over him, said "Though... I may need more bolts... it seems I might have used all the ones you bought me last week."

"Again! I..." she started to say, but then simply sighed. "Never mind, I shouldn't be surprised at this point. Shouldn't have told you we were going to the lake, should I. Oh well, I suppose you already thought about how to get this thing in the wagon haven't you?"

"Unlike your earlier assessment," Lapiutalnice confirmed, tapping his wrench on the main wing beam, "it isn't actually nailed into the frame, so the wings can be removed and reattached for transport. She should be able to fit into the wagon without issue... I just hope the horse is strong enough."

Nulaidutice sighed, "I'm sure he'll manage. I suppose you won't hurt yourself now, so I'll leave you to it. I need something to eat bad. Just don't use your leg, please, I don't want the commander to blame me for you being perpetually injured."

"I'll keep off of it, I owe you that much dear," he laughed as he kissed her cheek. "I made some bread for brunch, nothing fancy, but some butter should help spruce it up a bit."

"The first smart thing you've said all day," Nulaidutice razzed as she got back up to her feet, wiping the dirt off her dress. Then she walked her way out of the barn, leaving Lapiutalnice alone with his machine. For a moment he simply sat there, glad that there hadn't been much of a fuss in bringing his machine to the lake with them, as he didn't have a better idea of how to test the device. As usual, despite her complaints, his wife was more than accommodating toward his little schemes.

"At least until she finds out I ate the rest of the almonds with the bread," he remarked out loud to himself, "There is no forgiveness for that cardinal crime." Then, scooching himself forward with the wrench he got back to work fitting the metal struts under the wooden beams. If the Lapudrum was going to fly, he needed to get working – it wouldn't build itself after all.

2 The Visit

"I see you've made progress at your mad attempt to join us in the sky," came a crowing voice from behind the elf man who was hunched over his machine. He stopped with the ratchet mid-turn as he whipped his face around to smile at the new-comer.

"Piqoug!" he greeted the shadow at the barn door ecstatically, stumbling as he tried to raise himself without using his broken leg. "I'm glad you stopped by, I'm nearly finished with her! Isn't the Lapudrum a beauty?" Grinning, the elf gestured toward the device laying uncovered now in the center of the barn as he wiped the sawdust from his glasses. He had been working for the greater part of the morning, and was more than prepared to show off his project to someone.

"She certainly is…" the shadow started as he entered the shade of the dusty building, "… something, I'll give you that. I think calling it a sky boat was a good idea, it might as well be a flying kayak." Once his form was out of the brilliant sunlight the fact that he was not an elf became far more obvious. All but his yellow scaly hands and feet were covered in black feathers, and his clothes were not the typical elvish fashion. While his pointy-eared friend wore a belted blue shirt and some very dirty pants from scooching around the barn floor for hours, the bird man wore a tunic wrapped in colorful cloths with the patterns of his home aerie on Laetail, one of the oldest in the world.

Though far from his island roost, the harpy was not an infrequent visitor. Setting down the large sack of mail which had brought him to the region to begin with, he stretched his arms which were weary from flying all morning like his elf friend's were from working. "I would suggest you take a break so we could grab some lunch, but I can tell you're too excited to wait on this one," Piqoug stated bluntly as he crossed his arms in front of his massive muscular chest. To someone unaccustomed to reading his stern downy face with large black and seemingly uncaring eyes, he may have come off as annoyed or uninterested. Whether the elf man could see past his friend's appearance to his true feelings, or whether he was too oblivious to care, was certainly up for debate.

"I definitely stole a few ideas from the selkies," the elf man admitted excitedly, addressing the kayak comment. "Their designs are light and sleek, which I need if I want to get this thing airborne. I just used wood for the frame instead of bone. I could have used some leather for the main body instead of cloth, but it was becoming an expensive project as it is and I didn't want Nulai to panic out too much. Thus compromises were made, but she should still be sturdy enough."

As the elf was speaking, the bird man had approached the side of the device where one of the broad square wings lay in the straw. Plucking at one of the flaps at the back end, he turned a cocked head toward his friend, which Lapiutalnice learned was something like a raised eyebrow to the harpy, and asked, "What are these things? I certainly don't have any on my wings."

"That's because your wings are made up of many interlocking feathers that can be moved up and down to adjust your pitch and yaw," Lapiutalnice excitedly explained as he hobbled over to where his friend stood. "The wings of the Lapudrum aren't able to move like that, they mostly exist to create lift, so instead I rigged these flaps to simulate the same effect. They are kind of like the rudders of this sky boat if you will."

"I think I understand your meaning," the harpy said slowly. "I'll need to see it in action before I believe such rigid wings would do any good."

"I took your advice to think of her as a soaring machine rather than a flying machine," the elf man continued, pushing his still-dirty glasses further up his pointed nose. "Would you mind extending your wing for a better explanation?" Complying, the bird man reached down to what looked like a long loose sleeve that had been hanging down his side. But as he gripped the black feather folds and extended his arm out, his scaly hands disappeared into the sleek black flight feathers which unfurled from his side. Almost magically his arm was replaced by a gigantic wing, their broad tips fading from black to gray as they went, a beautiful and powerful appendage for flight.

"When you soar, you allow your wings to rest flat, correct?" the elf framed as a question but said more like a statement. "This allows the air currents to keep you up rather than expending all your energy flapping your wings."

"You have no idea how much of a relief it is to get that high up," Piqoug replied, making something similar to a sighing noise. "Take-offs leave you so tired."

"I'll bet," Lapiutalnice agreed quickly, before moving on with the explanation. "Now move your feathers as if you were going to try to raise yourself higher while soaring. And pay attention to how you do it, I know flying is second nature to you, but it is not natural to us elves obviously."

After a few seconds of fidgeting with his wing to mimic the processes he went through while flying, a little light seemed to come on in the dark pupils of eyes. "I see what you're doing now," he chirped happily as he let his flight feathers fall back to dangling from his arms. "Very clever, and that will work very well once you're already in the sky. But that is not going to get you up there unless you plan to drop the thing off a cliff."

"That is as much the hard part for me as it is for you, my friend," conceded the elf man, running his hands through his wild brown hair as he thought. "According to Nulai's math, she should take off if we get the machine going fast enough. Like someone running with a kite. The issue is, this is a very heavy kite, so we'll need to be going very fast."

"I don't think I can help you there," chuckled the harpy standing beside him as they both looked on at the strange device. "I've never tried to takeoff with my wings stiff as boards, nor do I really think I want to."

"I have some ideas," Lapiutalnice replied, though the cheer in his voice was dissipating. "Nulai has said that she's not confident that any of them will work, and everyone else I've brought it up to has been less kind to my ego. The consensus seems to be that it's impossible with our current technology."

"And of course they probably also said you're wasting your time and will never come up with anything," Piqoug groaned. "Elves have no imagination. If I had a copper leaf for every time elvish data told me something was impossible and later found out dwarvish experimentation had achieved the feat in the most moronic way conceivable, I could probably retire to being a nesttender." Shaking his head, the bird man continued, "Did you know they actually have flying devices? The Peks have literally weaponized the same hot air that fills their heads to push themselves skyward. Which is slow and not very practical for what you're trying, but they use them mostly for signaling anyway. Point is, I hope you succeed here, my friend, not just so you could accompany me on boring flights, but also to force those knuckleheads to grow a spine and try something for once. Elves have so much theoretical knowledge, it'd be great if they'd just use it for once!"

"We do," Lapiutalnice responded with the hyperbole of the statement sailing clear over his head. "Do you see dwarves with the printing press, guns, sailing ships, and what not? Flirting with Lady Luck like I do is not considered wise nor practical, however, and if there is one thing my colleagues hate it is impracticality. Right now they can't see a way to get this thing off the ground, so what's the point of making something that can soar?"

"At least they could have the decency to try," grumbled the bird as the sound of hooves came up the road toward the house behind them. "A lack of propulsion certainly didn't stop dwarvish thrill-seekers. But I suppose there isn't enough fun in the minds of most elves to try and power a flying machine on thick-headedness. This is why you're the only elf I hang out with, Lapiu. All the rest of my drinking buddies live around the nest or are humans out west."

"Well, it sounds like you might have a second one here soon," the elf man whispered quietly as they could faintly hear a knock at the door to his empty house. "I see they can't just trust me to come back and have to make sure I'm not fit for service."

"I mean, they can't really, can they?" Piqoug laughed as what was likely an elf soldier began calling for his hiding colleague. "Should I go grab him for you?"

Lapiutalnice waved the offer aside as he used the Lapudrum as a support to sink back down to the ground. "No, just let him be. If we don't acknowledge him, maybe he'll give up." Unfortunately for him, the other elf was persistent and came looking around the premises until he found his target, sitting moodily on the ground and making a far greater show of his leg than the soldier would have gotten an impression of if he had found him a few minutes earlier.

"There you are, Private Fienlapus," the soldier in the dark beige uniform said with some relief. "I was sent to check on the mending of your leg. I take it that it's still bothering you."

"It's been less than a week," Lapiutalnice replied coldly, his glare making no attempts to hide his opinion about the visit. His stony reception didn't seem to bother the Gaité soldier, however, as he knelt by his fellow conscript and put down his medical bag. Piqoug's presence seemed to confuse him more, but the soldier didn't comment on the feathery man as he went about his work. Raising Lapiutalnice's pant leg, he revealed a thick network of bandages and braces. Feeling around it and causing his fellow to grimace, the medic finally stood back up and made some notes on his clipboard.

After a moment he stated the obvious: "Still seems pretty bad. Make sure you stay off of it, finding you in the barn every time we visit is concerning." With his business concluded, the brown haired fellow picked his bag back up and turned to leave his comrade and the exasperated harpy alone. But he was stopped by a glance over at the nearly complete flying machine. He remained silent for a few seconds, as if his curiosity and sense were dueling it out to figure if it was a good idea to ask about it or not.

Much to the bird's surprise, it was the curiosity that won out this time, as he asked, "Is it close to flying then, Private Fienlapus?"

"Close to being tested soon," he said carefully, making sure he left out the details about him doing said testing. "But as has been said many times, I still haven't come up with an engine for it."

"That's why it's best to leave such things to the learned women," the elf replied with such a straight face it was hard to believe he had shot his colleague down so hard. "But still, if Nulaidutice ever does help you come up with one, I'm sure the commander will be very interested. Not to mention the ladies down in Paipadaívaen. This could be the turning point in our bloody stalemate with Teulyakeo. But it ain't a shot I'd bet on." With that he marched straight out of the barn, and a few seconds later they heard the sound of hoof beats leaving the two in peace again.

"That's what I'm afraid of," the elf man finally said as he leaned back against his project.

The harpy ruffled his feathers in such a way that the elf man had found was similar to a snort. "Don't pay attention to him. Missing a shot isn't such a big deal. Better than not taking it at all. You elves live so long anyway, a few wasted months shouldn't even register to you."

"Not that," Lapiutalnice waved his black-feathered friend's encouragement aside. "The sunk cost fallacy has already sunk in far too deep to abandon this now. I'm far more concerned with how the commander is going to respond if I actually succeed."

"I see," was all the bird man said as he looked out the door where the soldier had left them. For now, the military was turning their backs on the Lapiutalnice while they thought his plans and goals were absurd. Yet if he proved them wrong, they would be hopping all over this. Piqoug had known the young elf for his entire career, having met him before he transferred over into the Daechûg, and knew he'd like nothing more than to be free of those shackles. He wasn't a warrior, though few elves were; he had a gentle spirit that even gave sympathy to the orcs which would probably rip him apart if they had the chance. He knew that flight, to him, was as much an escape from the Gaité as it was from the ground. The dream was the only thing keeping him from hating his life.

Of course, the harpy never said any of this. It didn't need to be. Still, the silence was only growing, and Piqoug thought he could hear his stomach in the still, stuffy air of the barn, so he lowered a taloned claw to help his friend back onto his feet. "Well, you can't prove that jerk wrong without some food in your stomach. I know you don't eat a ton, but flying makes me famished and I want to eat before I go back to my runs. I've got a few leaves somewhere around here, probably near the Trulpanun coils, lunch can be on me this time. Then Nulaidutice won't threaten to make a roast pheasant out of me for eating the hazelnut stash again."

Laughing, Lapiutalnice took his friend's hand, and his twig-like form lifted easily off the ground, "She's rather ferocious, isn't she? Messing with her stash is the quickest way to find her temper."

"Still not sure exactly what all the ruckus is about nuts," Piqoug shook his head as he helped support his friend while they walked down toward the nearest coffeehouse in the tiny town, "Now, some fish sounds good. But I will probably have to settle for rabbit in this hell-hole. Why did you ever move from the coast, my friend?"

The elf man laughed, his spirits looking high again. "Believe me, it wasn't my choice!" he chuckled, and off they went down the dirt road. The scorching heat of the afternoon was about ready to start, which of course would conveniently trap them in Natniln until Nulaidutice came by with the cart and brought the two back. How could they have planned their day so poorly? A question she would likely never receive a convincing answer to.

3 The Sunset

It was strange for Lapiutalnice to just sit back and enjoy the afternoon for a change. While he could still be found gazing up at the sky, this time it was from the back porch of their small stubby house rather than the barn. The sweltering cave in which he had been toiling for the past few days to meet the lake trip deadline. The sun could get fairly hot out in Daechûg, even though they were almost as far north as Faitalgie stretched – the nearest sea to them was miles away to the east or the west. They lived at the bare edge of habitability, at least that's what the elf man thought as he longed for the cool ocean breezes of his homeland.

But the shade from the broad-roofed dwelling helped mitigate the damage, and the jar trap full of rotting leftovers from the night before helped mitigate the insects, so he was not all that angry with the situation. He did not envy the orcs however, who lived in this heat out on the steppe all summer with no warm house to retreat to in the winter. And yet, judging by the horn calls over the past few days, they were doing fine; Nulaidutice even told him how a whole clan passed by Natniln yesterday! So she had heard, at least.

"Still think we don't need to worry about the grayskins?" she had asked jokingly, knowing exactly how her husband would respond. He didn't disappoint by asking if they were hurting anything and was simply met with the confirmation, "Nope, only got close enough to scare us. As usual once they saw the Gaités they turned back toward the mountains. Their flocks of goats and alpacas looked like a sea according to the ladies I was speaking with, though. They were rather frightened, swearing their numbers must be growing out there."

Always the same response – this was why he was hiding behind his house rather than in front of it. For one thing, there was more shade, but for another, he didn't want to talk to anyone about the recent events. The last major orc attacks had been centuries ago, before the Gaités had been built, and yet that was all anyone talked about when he'd been on duty. Orcs rarely even lived half a century, according to his wife; more likely than not those orcs who last attacked would have been the great-grandparents of the clan which passed Natniln the day before. If not, further removed.

A lot can change in that amount of time, and these orcs were probably told to be afraid of those dorky wooden cubes by their parents, just like Lapiutalnice was told to be afraid whenever he saw a wave of sheep on the horizon. No he'd rather not be roped into gossip and worry, he'd rather enjoy the clouds and daydream about his project. Wouldn't have minded a book, too, but he'd read all the interesting textbooks from Nulaidutice's college years several times already. He'd have to be content with the sky.

It never ceased to be enjoyable to him – the sky was constantly changing, the large puffy clouds of the region constantly reshaping and morphing for his amusement, and of course the sun was on its continual march. It was late now, hidden behind the slate shingles that spared him from the heat, and soon it would be painting those clouds fun colors as it set in the west. He was ready for the evening to come so that the night could follow, filling the sky with brilliant stars, and then the morning would come, and the trip to the lake.

His wild device was wrapped up in canvas on the back of the cart already, which would make his wife rather upset when she got home. He had been too excited to wait, though, and spent the earlier parts of the day disassembling the device and reassembling her in the wagon for transport. It was probably more taxing of an activity than he should have undertaken with his leg, but he was too excited to think of anything else. After that, it was a quick round of their animals, giving special attention to the horse, and now he had exhausted his chores, simply enjoying his tea in the waning light.

Much earlier than expected, he heard the sound of hooves on the road behind the house, hinting to his wife's arrival. Sure enough, he heard the horse and cart stop, followed by some thanks to her friend who had given her a lift and his wife rounding the corner of the house. Her hair being tied back into a halo today revealed that the sun had done a number on her. Face red and peeling, she must have been neglecting the wide-brimmed hat slung behind her head, as usual. This made the elf man roll his eyes as he was thinking about the lecture he was going to get for using his leg all morning. Lapiutalnice was going to enjoy pointing out the hypocrisy of it all, but he'd let her start it.

She didn't seem that interested in any talking, however, and simply collapsed in the chair beside her husband, grabbing his tea from the table and draining it in one long swig. He couldn't help but laugh as he watched his wife guzzle down his drink, her face still scrunched in discomfort from the heat and face coated in sweat. He hadn't looked much better a few hours ago, but sitting on the covered porch had done wonders. The white chipped paint gleamed ominously at the edge of the long eave, but beyond that was blissful shadow and a mild southern breeze from the forest.

She would probably be better before they entered the house in the evening, though they would not dare enter that furnace any sooner. He could practically see the heat radiating from the dark yawning portal into their humble abode. Nulaidutice also gazed toward it as if gauging whether it was worth heading in to get another bottle of the life-saving liquid, but eventually decided against it. Instead, she simply hitched up her teal dress to release some of the heat and closed her eyes in relief as the breeze washed over her legs.

"Long day at work, I take it," Lapiutalnice said as he saw his wife finally seem to get comfortable.

She didn't answer for a moment, simply enjoying the chance to cool down, but eventually turned toward him, the freckles on her face returning as the red faded. "Well I did get off early, but yes thanks for noticing," she said wiping her brow. "The new laborers barely knew how to set up a crossbeam, I practically had to do it for them. Sometimes I think we should let men go to school to at least teach you morons which side of the hammer you hit with. Also take that shirt off, I'm dying watching you wear it."

"Oh, what would the ladies say?" he teased as he pulled off his brown over-shirt, his twig-like form much more prominent without the baggy extra layer. "We're out on the porch and everything."

In response she stuck her tongue out at her husband, but was still too busy dying to retaliate. Chuckling, the elf man got up and grabbed a paper fan they kept on the windowsill for her. Gratefully Nulaidutice began fanning more air into her stinging face, finally getting comfortable enough to continue talking. "Why did we ever take the steppe from the orcs? This place is death. Your house is either baking you alive or your well is frozen."

"Aw but, Nulai, the oats grow so well out here!" her husband laughed as he stood behind his wife and massaged her shoulders, "The forest transitional zone was absolutely wasted by those barbarians. Besides, something about keeping the woodlands safe, make the Plains Elves deal with orc raids instead, political nonsense, the lake is nice, etcetera."

Laughing, the elf woman leaned her head back to look up into the impish face of the man behind her. "Can't keep your mind on the here and now, can you? It's either wandering around among the clouds or out on that bloody lake."

"Well as you kindly pointed out earlier, there isn't much here, is there?" he retorted. "Especially in the hot months, just dead grass and lines of sad-looking trees."

"I'm here!" Nulaidutice punched at her husband in mock offense. "You could pay attention to me."

"Is what I'm doing now not enough, your majesty," he laughed as he rolled his eyes. "I've gotten you your fan, I didn't even complain when you drank the rest of my tea. It's far too early to think about cooking you dinner, what more could I do for you, my lady?"

"Oh, I can think of a few things," the elf woman said as she smirked into the distance. "I'll save those for later, though. Right now maybe you could... stay off your leg, idiot! Did you get your entire bloody machine in the cart while I was gone?" With that Lapiutalnice couldn't help but laugh hysterically as his wife glared at the loaded cart. "Do you want to be in pain for our entire lake trip, because if your leg isn't killing you I will!" The threat was only met with further fits of laughter as the elf man held onto the back of his wife's chair to keep himself from collapsing to the floor.

"Lapiu, what am I going to do with you?" she groaned as she got to her feet and forcibly sat her husband back in his chair. "I had just told the commander what a good boy you were being, playing around with your carpentry tools in the barn to keep you busy."

"Used those exact words, did you?" the elf man managed to get out between fits of giggles, grasping his chest to try and calm down his breathing. She simply raised an eyebrow at him and snorted.

"Like the ladies need more fuel for their gossip," she sighed in mock exasperation. "They all know you're up to something. Once they figure out how much I'm facilitating these silly dreams they're going to have a heyday."

"Not ready to be that popular, are you?" the elf man replied with some sarcasm, but he also took his wife's hand as he did. She didn't seem worried about it yet. She was a strong woman, however; it would take a lot to get to her.

To confirm his suspicion that there may be concern behind her confidence, Nulaidutice simply shrugged in response, the bold veneer breaking a bit as she sat down on the arm rest of her husband's chair. "They already think I'm crazy, might as well let them know I am. I'm the only girl at work who doesn't think it the highest honor to work on the Gaités. Like those wooden cubes are hard to make. The men probably could, once they figure out which end of the hammer is up."

"Maybe they'll put you on housing duty next," her husband tried to say encouragingly as they watched the clouds grow red as the sun set down over the sea far, far away. "That at least is a little more interesting and involved. You can make it elegant and not just resistant to orcish axes."

"You know how the Plains Elves are, dear," she sighed sadly. "They are allergic to elegance. Everything must be hardy and practical." As she said that she glowered back at their square house, faint blue paint peeling from many winters of weather abuse. "And besides, that's for the architects, not engineers like me. They don't have fancy gates or dugouts in a house."

"Still, my point remains," Lapiutalnice continued, squeezing his wife's hand. "You're brain is far bigger than the Gaité. I just wish someone besides me would see that."

She laughed in response, "You're not doing a very good at convincing them, love. If my husband invents flying machines before I do, I'll be the disgrace of all women." She said it as a joke, but the elf man knew the tight-rope she was walking was far narrower than she let on.

"You basically did," he said quietly, leaning against her as he watched the brilliantly colored clouds move and change. "You've done all the math, after all, I'm just putting the thing together."

"Leave me out of this," she said with a smile, her fingers absentmindedly running through his wild brown hair. "This whole thing was your idea. I can't be faulted if I do a little math for a cute face like that. Might even be able to keep my dignity being married to you with that excuse."

"An elf falling for a cute face," the elf man chuckled. "What would the ladies say?" At that point they both went quiet, though, having had enough flirting with the potential crisis on the horizon. Besides, tomorrow was the lake, and he didn't want to spoil the mood too much. Slowly the hazy air began to calm down and cool off, the dusty baked earth ceasing to radiate the warmth of the sun back into the air as its rays dissipated beyond the horizon.

Before the light was entirely gone, the Fienlapus retreated into their abode, entering into the main room of the square house they both hated so much. The fireplace and oven sat off to one side, where traditionally the table would also be located. Nulaidutice had dragged theirs over to the window on the other side, however, partially as an act of rebellion and partially so she could have sunlight while she drafted out projects. Her husband never complained, as the view of the sky was far better than the walls of the room. They needed to repaint the beige walls something awful, and the lumpy blue sofa his mother had forced upon him was far from his favorite thing. That's why they buried it under as many coats as they could, their actual coat rack being filled with his wife's hats, their wide brims layered on top of one another to the point where taking one off was a hazard.

After the straw one she had been pretending to wear that day was added to the collection, the elf woman began to busy about the oven to get it ready for cooking. Each time Lapiutalnice tried to get up out of his chair to try and prevent the imminent disaster that was his wife's cooking, he was met with the point of a knife from across the room. "Stay off the leg, you've put enough pressure on it for one day, I'm sure," she'd say as she busied around the fire. It was still a little warm to be baking, but they wanted to get up early the next morning, so waiting further into the evening wasn't a grand idea.

"I want to get out of Natniln before anyone is watching to ask about the extra load," was her excuse, but her husband suspected she was as excited to get to the lake as he was. It was as much an escape for her as it was for him, after all, and the Lady of Labor knew she needed a vacation… though maybe not as frequently as she took them, of course. Not that he would complain.

Talk about the "extra load" lasted for the rest of the meal. Lapiutalnice wanted to make sure he wasn't forgetting anything, and his wife wanted to know just how much of a fool she would seem before this was all done. He assured her that that if it didn't work, they'd be far out on the lake, and only the other sailors would be paying attention at that point. Judging by the raised eyebrows and doubtful noises she made in between mouthfuls of overcooked oat bread and cheese, she was not convinced. However, she also didn't protest, so the elf man continued to run with the plan, hoping to get him and his wife onto the water before her better judgment kicked in.

"It will basically be a normal trip," he said as the elf woman sitting across the table from him assisted in finishing off his portion of bread. "We'll just be dragging the Lapudrum behind us as we sail. If all goes well she should look like a kite of sorts."

"Oh boy," Nulaidutice mumbled through a mouthful of oats that had recently been joined by a large portion of hot tea. "It looks so much better that my husband is playing with kites. You don't need to convince the world that you're childish. They already know."

"Then I don't have to pretend otherwise either," he said happily as he got up to start clearing the table. This was met with a stern look, so he changed course, making his way slowly toward the bedroom. "No use in trying to hide something everyone else is already convinced of."

"At least then I could say you're trying to grow up," his wife replied as she dumped the cloth and cups into the basin haphazardly, where Lapiutalnice knew they'd be waiting for them when they got back. This made him chuckle – she'd make a terrible husband, but then again, he wasn't one to talk.

"You'd be bored if I was sane," he snarked back from the bedroom door as she went to pour the rest of the kettle into bottles to drink on their excursion. "What other husband would bring up such fun topics like torsion and aerodynamics?" His own comment backfired in his head, though, and immediately he drifted off thinking about his main conundrum. "I do wonder how I'd get that thing going," he murmured to himself, but his wife's pointy ears were keen and picked it up anyway. Quickly she hurried over to diffuse the thought before they lost more hours to physics talk.

"Not tonight, doofus," she said, pushing her husband into their bedroom with a slight smirk on her face, "that's enough about flying boats for one evening. Or one week, but that's not happening with the lake tomorrow."

"I do suppose it is finally past sundown," Lapiutalnice conceded, looking out the window toward the shadowy landscape absentmindedly. "I just wish I could think of a proper energy source. Without anyway to gain and maintain speed this will all be for nothing."

"Yeah, well, unlike your dorky ship, I have energy to spare tonight," his wife said, lighting a reed candle on her desk and turning to face him. The shadows filled the corners of her angular face, but he could tell it wore that amused look she always had around him. Closing the distance between them, she wrapped her slender arms around his waist. Inwardly Lapiutalnice found himself sighing – he hoped it wasn't going to be one of those nights.

Pulling her husband closer, Nulaidutice's glittering eyes appeared in the candlelight as she looked up at him. "Is tonight the night Lapiu?" she whispered, pressing in against him tightly. Before he could answer she leaned forward to meet him in a kiss, one that she dragged out as long as she could. He could tell that she anticipated his reaction, which made him laugh inwardly but also saddened him. He would give her the same answer he did every time she insinuated a child, but he had been giving that excuse for several decades now. He was beginning to wonder how much longer she was willing to wait.

Upon releasing his face and seeing the mixed emotions there, he watched the hungry light rapidly leave his wife's eyes. "Still a no, then," she said as she abruptly dropped her arms and turned back around toward the wardrobe. "I see that stupid sky boat of yours is still more important than my dignity."

"I hadn't said anything yet, nor will I," Lapiutalnice laughed, though with some nervousness. "I can go grab a muzzle cover from the drawer if you want." She merely snorted something about it being late anyway as she pulled a nightgown out from the wardrobe and sat it on top for safe-keeping as she undressed for bed. He noted the rather teasing way she went about the task, despite attraction not being the issue here. He shook his head quietly as he too began to pull off his plain undershirt and grab his own night robes from the bedside drawer. Considering that he didn't have an audience, he redressed much faster, ready to greet his wife with a raised eyebrow when she turned back around in her night clothes.

"They accuse you of holding out on me, you know," Nulaidutice said dryly, putting her hands on her hips. "I was told to take another husband yesterday, just so someone would give me children." They had been through this song and dance enough times for Lapiutalnice to know the scowl she wore was not deeply felt, but he wondered if it was penetrating deeper each time he postponed the future of her family.

"Well, you've heard my reasoning, but as the wife that decision really belongs to you, dear," he chuckled nervously as he tried to humor his way out of the situation again. "Lecture me, tell me how its for the good of our community and needed to bolster the ranks, whatever rot the empress is peddling these days. Go on, you know I'm an obedient and good husband, I will listen to my learned wife." With his tongue-and-cheek attack on her femininity mounted, he crawled under the covers to sleep. He could just barely make out a tired smile at the edge of the lamp-light, confirming his appeal had worked. He was fortunate that she played as fast and loose with their social duties as he did, but he wondered how long she would let him keep this up.

Though she lacked the usual bemusement in her eyes, she didn't press further. She simply went over and blew out the reed candle, plunging the room into the soft glow of the final rays of twilight. Though he could no longer see her, Lapiutalnice kept his eyes on the place where she had been, wondering what he did to have a wife who humored him so. Even as the covers lifted to admit her, he did not take his eyes off where she had stood, still sitting propped up on the pillows as she snuggled in close. He moved one of his arms absentmindedly to embrace her, resting his head on her bushy blonde hair.

"Lapiu," she muttered after awhile, her breath warm on his face, "do consider, though, that if I'm pregnant they'll give me leave from overseeing the construction. Then I can be home and help you with your air boat. Maybe we'd even be able to figure out a way to propel it forward before the child was old enough to justify me going back to work." The last few sentences were released with a yawn, though her grip only tightened as she spoke.

"With you helping, I have no doubt we'd have the Lapudrum in the air before the child sees her first decade," Lapiutalnice replied, finally closing his eyes as well. Once he did, they were filled with images of a small child, hair still short enough to expose their pointy ears underneath. The child sat before him in his beautiful creation, as they took off into the air, riding the wind like a kite. Higher and higher they went, flying up toward the sea of clouds and whatever else lay beyond the terrestrial world.

"I do not doubt it," he repeated, silent tears welling up behind firmly shut eyelids, "but you know I want it to be ready for them, something she may share in, not feel neglected because of. I will finish it first, then I promise I will give you a child. I promise."

Nulaidutice groaned dramatically, though sleep was coming

over her much more quickly than for her husband. "So we're never gonna have a kid. I'm going to be the laughing stock of the entire town, I hope you know that. Almost a century old and not a single kid," she said it in jest, but Lapiutalnice knew it was true. What if he never did get his mad dream airborne – when should he give in? What if it took several more centuries? How long would she put up with this? How long should she put up with this?

"She will fly," he finally whispered into the dark, more for his own benefit than hers. Which was good, as his comment was greeted with a snore. Being more than a little wrapped up in her sleeping gown now, he did not dare try and move to a more comfortable position; instead he stared wide-eyed into the darkness. From it crept his doubts and worries. Was it even possible, was everyone right and he just holding his wife back?

She didn't admit to even half of what was being said behind her back – he knew that everyone in Natniln thought he was crazy and wasting a brilliant woman's time. Often, as now, he too wondered why she put up with his antics. If he could not feel her slender fingers gripping him tightly even after she had gone to sleep, he might have doubted even then that she would keep him around. But he could not deny what he could feel with his senses, despite it making no actual sense.

Closing his eyes again, he fantasized about being up in the clouds, and with him was a young woman with a smug face and a tiny child excitedly watching the world go by far below. As the tears ran down his cheek, he knew he could not abandon this dream. He might lose everything, but what else did he have to gain? To be a pawn for the Gaité system for the rest of his life, doing nothing for Nulaidutice more than supplying her heirs? No, he owed her more than that, and though it was risky, it was the only way to pay off that debt. "She will fly," he whispered one final time as he drifted off to join his wife in the realm of dreams, his doubts put off until the first rays of dawn.

4 The Lake

"Don't you have work to do other than watch my husband make a fool of himself?" Nulaidutice sighed as she watched the spindly man clamber up and down the rig, trying to piece it together with all the grace of a one-man band on a frozen lake. Lapiutalnice had lost his glasses in the grass somewhere long ago and was simply squinting at struts to see if they were the correct ones. Even the horse seemed to be judging him as it stood there grazing.

"Perhaps, but this is rather entertaining," the bird man replied as they watched some locals approach the mess, probably to ask if the young man had hurt himself. "You don't suppose we should be helping, do you?"

"Nah, he's got it," the elf woman said as she took a swig of tea from her bottle. "Those poor farmers are about to be recruited whether they want to be or not. He may be a man, but he makes up for that with sheer enthusiasm."

"Looks like a bunch of field workers, probably got bored of tilling some lady's plantation and decided to join the fun," Piqoug concurred as he began to casually preen his dangling flight feathers. "Doesn't matter to them if he's crazy or not, they've lost nothing for their efforts." Sure enough, Lapiutalnice had built up a little task force behind him, the other elf men in their dirt-covered undershirts swarming the machine like ants as he called out instructions (meanwhile searching the grass for his glasses).

"Yep, so I'm just gonna watch from over here judgmentally until he asks me to get in the boat with him," she replied, sinking back into the collapsible chair she had brought. "No need to forfeit my dignity until I have to."

"I don't know, this dignity thing seems rather dumb to me, those men seem to be having way move fun," the black-feathered man replied genuinely as he crossed his arms to keep his wings from billowing in the gathering wind. But then he looked down at the freckled elf woman who gave him a wink out from under the boater that she desperately was trying to keep on her head.

"Why do you think I married him? Certainly was not to build up my reputation," she snorted.

"That's good," Piqoug replied, watching the men awkwardly fighting the wind as they tried to flip the assembled Lapudrum right side up, attracting the glowers of a group of woman walking down the path past them. "If you had I'd be suggesting a replacement."

"Ha, mothers aren't going to offer me their respectable men at this point, I lost that chance long ago," she chuckled until she saw her husband waving in their direction with his posse of workers chattering behind him. "At least he could have the sense to wait until the other ladies had moved past though," she grumbled as she pulled her blue-trimmed hat down over her face to hide from the looks the walkers were giving her. "This might be a long afternoon."

"Well I'll have fun at least," smirked the harpy as he began to wander over to his friend across the way. "Should be interesting to see your wingless attempt at flight." He didn't go far, though, because Lapiutalnice hadn't waited for his crew to join them, but had ridden the wind to where they were sitting despite his bad leg.

"Got some help, so it all went rather quickly," he said happily, too excited to sound proud of himself or even grateful. He had one thought on his mind and that was to get his machine out over the water.

"Well good for you, dear," Nulaidutice said dryly are she took another swig of tea from her bottle. "I take it you aren't going to spare me the embarrassment and let me watch with your new-found audience if you're over here then."

"No, I need you to man the boat," he replied quickly, ignoring his wife's feigned lack of enthusiasm. "I'm going to be sitting in the Lapudrum to steer her, otherwise she'll probably roll midair and crash even if we get going fast enough."

"And how fast do expect me to get this boat going?" she said, raising her eyebrows at her husband. This was the first time the giddy childlike look on his face faltered, being replaced by a hesitant but determined expression.

"Well," he said slowly, enduring his wife's intense gaze as he formulated his thoughts, "it will need to be going faster than usual. The wind should help both the boat and the Lapudrum stay airborne. But the fact that the boat will need to be riding with the wind and not into will make it harder..."

"How fast, dear?" she interrupted, her eyebrows never lowering as she stared him down.

He paused a second, then sighing, he replied bluntly, "Twenty knots if the wind keeps up."

This was enough to make his wife blink. "You want me to do twenty knots on a lake while towing you behind me. You are insane."

"Well," he remarked timidly, "it would have been faster if the wind wasn't good. But it usually is so I was counting on that..."

"They barely can make those speeds on the open sea, Lapiu," Nulaidutice groaned as she stood to her feet, hat firmly in hand to keep it from surrendering to the wild wind that was their only hope. "What kind of boat do you think we have out here? It's a casual sailing vessel, not an Island Elf scouting ship!"

"But if you lean in with the wind and tighten the sails, going north up the shore..." her husband began before being abruptly cut off.

"We might be able to do twenty knots." Though her exasperation was growing she did give her husband a hand down toward the docks where their boat was waiting, the intrigued farmhands pushing the strange device behind them so it could be firmly tethered to the waiting seacraft. "Might be able to do twenty knots if Lady Luck smiles on us and Wisdom hides her face in embarrassment," she added quickly to make sure not to get Lapiutalnice's hopes up.

Unfortunately for her, his hope, or perhaps his obsession, would not be swayed so easily. "Lady Luck has always smiled upon me, the proof of that is standing right in front of me," he grinned, taking his wife's hands as they stood before their moored boat, one that looked a little small to be pulling twenty knots. "I'm willing to tempt her again, as long as her first gift is willing to go along with it."

This finally got his wife's face to crack – she dropped her bewilderment and allowed her typical amused expression to return. "I'm just along for the ride, dork, if this thing doesn't fly, it's not my problem. I'm just happy to be away from the Gaité."

Absolutely giddy with excitement, the elf man tried to help raise her over the side of the ship rail. "I don't know what I did to make Luck so happy, but even if she doesn't smile on me today, I can't complain. I've taken more gifts from her than I can afford!"

"It's 'cause you're a gigantic flirt," Nulaidutice laughed, stopping her husband from hurting himself and climbing over the railing, where she finally stowed her wide-brimmed hat in her handbag. "The poor Lady probably can't help herself. You have a knack for getting us to act fairly human sometimes. Now go get in your stupid flying machine, Piqoug is already circling up there waiting for you!"

Lapiutalnice didn't need to be told twice – he quickly hobbled to the back end of the boat where the other men had just finished securing the Lapudrum. After thanking them profusely, the elf woman watched with a smirk as her husband clambered into the strange wooden device with rigid cloth wings. They were about to attempt what no rational mind would ever do, and thus no elf had ever tried. It was time to prove that those born without wings could fly.

Turning to the sails, Nulaidutice swiftly got them into place to catch the wind and pulled them close to taunt. Hopefully it would be enough to carry them, but twenty knots was very fast. Lady Luck had better be as amused with her husband as she was if they were going to achieve takeoff. But his confidence was wearing off on her, so she strode back to the wheel and looked back to where that starry-eyed idiot was getting ready.

After she had gotten the blonde tangles out her face, she was able to see the young man giving a thumbs up from his sky boat, ready for whatever would come. Returning the gesture, she turned to the rudder and positioned it to lead them away from the other moored ships and out into the open waters of the lake. The vast body of water waiting for them, and once she had gotten some distance from the shore, she turned into the wind.

Now, with it directly to her back, she truly felt like there might be a chance. The wind was so strong today it felt like the sails would fly off the mast! She felt as if she might take off herself, and judging by the wake, her boat might have already been pulling ten knots or so, a good lead. They would have to wait and see if it would get any faster than that.

Looking back, she could barely make out the Lapudrum through her fluttering hair. The rope was taut and the machine bounced on the wake, but it was still raising a spray to match her own, and thus was obviously not flying. She would need to be going faster to get that tub in the air, something she wasn't sure she could pull off. Ten knots was already a lot, but she adjusted the sails and turned the boat more directly into the wind, hoping the Lady of Wisdom wasn't laughing too hard at her. Though, they were bold enough to sail in this gale, so she was surely shaking her head a little bit. At least it was keeping other, wiser, sailors off the lake and giving Nulaidutice the space she needed.

To her side, the black-winged bird came gliding in, Piqoug's bag in his talons behind him to help reduce the drag as he soared alongside the ship. Riding the gale up to the helm came his cry, like the scream of a falcon on the wind rather than the words of elves. Two long and a short, he was directing her to the right, she suddenly realized, remembering the little pieces of harpy signaling her husband had relayed to her. Accepting his far greater attunement to the wind, she adjusted the rudder a little more to the left, allowing the ship to swing into the desired position, then almost fell over as the ship lurched into action.

The excited screech of the bird man was almost drowned out by the roar of the wind and spray as the ship took off down the shoreline. Amazed, she realized they might actually be pulling twenty knots now, or close to it. Her dress was getting soaked by stray foam, and her hair frustratingly obscured her vision, yet she added her own whoop of wild abandon to that of the harpy's. Even if the bloody boat didn't fly, she at least would have a good time. Just as she was getting the soggy strands of hair out of her eyes, she felt the shadow of great wings fall over her, and onto the deck Piqoug stumbled, clearly coasting out of a dive as he rolled across the planks.

"I can't keep up anymore," he shouted as he clung to the mast for support, his wings now hanging limp from his arms and flapping wildly in the wind. "I don't know how you did it, but you've got to be going fast enough now!"

"I doubt I can go any faster, this is what the doofus is getting," Nulaidutice yelled back, her voice only audible thanks to the bird being down wind. "I'm surprised we haven't lost the sail! If he needs me to be going faster that thing is never getting off the water..." She had been about to continue but was interrupted by the pointing fingers of the bird man. Judging by the look of amazement in his eye, something must be happening. Turning around, all the work she had done to manage her hair was undone, but she could barely make out that something was off. Beside her she felt the presence of Piqoug, his hands grasping the rudder to help keep it steady while she tried to pull her hair back, admitting defeat in the face of the roaring wind. Not much progress was made toward that, however, as the moment she had her hair gathered and could see again she let go in wonder. For behind them, hovering a span or two above the water, was the Lapudrum.

Resting uneasily on the rushing cushion of air, the canvas wings bulged upward, the speed of the boat pulling the device into the sky. It moved slowly up and down as if it couldn't decide whether to remain airborne or return to the lake, probably going as slow as it could go to gain lift, but still it hovered there. In the cockpit, just barely visible, was the waving brown hair of her husband, hands she guessed intently on the stick he used to steer the thing. Smirking, Nulaidutice waved back at the mad genius, though she knew he was too intent on his work to notice. She would tease him about being single minded later, but she fully understood being wrapped up in this work. She would be too if she were the first elf to fly!

"Can you take back the helm, Nulaidutice?" came the crowing voice from beside her. "I'm going to see if I can congratulate him while he is still in my realm." Nodding, she carefully took back the ship from Piqoug's scaly hands and watched as the harpy gripped his wings and flung them full. Seamlessly they merging with his arms – it was strange to her that only moments earlier they had been swinging like sleeves at his side, but now caught the full of the wind, allowing the bird man to take off like his elvish contemporary. Once above the deck he allowed himself to be outpaced by the rushing boat, drifting back to where Lapiutalnice was manning his own vessel.

The wonder of the situation never left her, though she had to watch where the ship was heading now rather than the groundbreaking feat behind her. They were going very fast, after all, and though they were far out in deep waters, there were a few other brave souls also taking advantage of the wind, and she had already traveled a great distance without paying attention. Fortunately she would not need to wait long for a report. Once again, using the speed of a dive to his advantage, Piqoug came tumbling onto the deck, laughing as he came crashing to the floor.

"That husband of yours is stiff as stone," he cackled. "He said he didn't get the steering quite right and he has to clench the stick to keep the Lapudrum from rolling back down into the lake. You can put away the sails, he's ready to land."

"That lily-livered husband of mine," she groaned in mock exasperation, but followed through on his request with the help of the harpy on board. Together they rolled up the sails, and the boat started to slow. With their work done, the elf woman turned back toward the other vessel, hands on hips, ready to tease his lack of spine. But it was her turn for her eyes to go wide as she saw the Lapudrum barreling toward her boat, still keeping the speed they had built up even though the boat was slowing. Acting fast, Piqoug rushed to the rudder and turned hard, using their remaining speed to pull out of the way. Behind them now the strange device came crashing back to the water almost on its side, causing it to crash onto the surface upside down, plunging her husband down with it.

"LAPIU," she screamed, all thoughts of sass leaving her as she kicked off her shoes and jumped into the wake to swim out toward the crash. Her dress got in the way of her swimming, but the movement of the boat helped drag the wreck of her husband's invention closer toward her. Riding the wind, the black-winged shadow came down upon the boat far faster than she did, though she could not tell what Piqoug was doing once perched upon the Lapudrum. It did not become clear until she was closer that there was a matted mop of brown hair and the white sleeves of an elvish undershirt clinging to the side of her husband's invention, and that the harpy was simply talking to his friend, laughing about the state of these affairs.

"Lapiutalnice, you idiot!" she growled as she pulled up next to him in the water, gripping her husband and his invention to give her tired arms and legs a break in the water. "I jumped into this ice-cold water to save you from drowning, and I find you laughing out here?"

Kissing his wife as they clung to the side of the Lapudrum, the elf man's only response was to laugh! He was still shaking from the excitement of the crash, but otherwise seemed fine. Soaked so thoroughly his normally baggy overtunic clung to his twig-like arms, and his face turning a bit blue, but otherwise unscathed. It took a long time to speak, but when he finally did, any fear he had while flying the machine was gone, replaced with wonder in his voice again. "I can die peacefully now, because I have flown," was his only comment as he bobbed up and down in the water, resting his head on his wife's shoulder as he gazed up once more into the clouds.

"Oh, that was barely flying," Piqoug waved away the statement with a taloned hand, "I have no doubt you'll get this thing truly airborne if you managed to do that with a boat and some good wind. All you need is something to pull it like the boat did, but faster..." Lapiutalnice's raised eyebrow was enough to stop his friend right there and cause him to laugh. "Alright, fair, finding something faster and as strong as a speeding boat will be hard."

"He'll figure out something, though," Nulaidutice continued, with a rather more supportive tone than usual. "He's way too headstrong not to." Her husband made no reply, however, and simply let her stroke his soaking brown hair as he floated along, watching the clouds.

"Alright, dreamer boy, get your head back down to earth," she smirked, rolling her eyes, "I'm gonna need your help swimming back to the ship. My dress was not the right choice for saving your life in." And sure enough it was no help getting them to swim back to the boat, especially since it was drifting away from them this time rather than toward. But with Piqoug waiting to help them back onboard when they got there, it didn't take them long to turn the boat around and start making their way back to shore, zigzagging their way slowly against the wind as they did.

With the going so slow they saw the crowd gathered on the

shore long before they reached them. It had grown from the small team of farmhands who'd helped Lapiutalnice assemble his flying machine to a rather large gathering. Even from afar they could see added to the farmhands the beige uniforms of Gaité soldiers and the colorful dresses of women mixed in. Apparently either word had spread, or more eyes were looking out on the lake than they had expected. As they neared the crowded docks they could hear the cheers of the men, swarming like ants to receive their cold and soaking heroes at port.

"Looks like you've got a crowd of fans already," Nulaidutice grinned as she waved to the enthusiastic gathering. But then she looked toward her husband and saw his face solemn by comparison, and underneath that was concern. "Don't worry Lapiu," she continued, hugging him close as the soldiers and farmhands grabbed the ropes Piqoug tossed to them and began tying them to the shore, "they'll have to take you seriously now. Even the High Elves in Tivowichaisch from the City of a Thousand Trees will be hearing about the Sea Elf from nowhere who flew."

"That's what I'm afraid of," was his only response before they were swarmed by the crowd excited to meet the first elf to fly.

5 The Dinner Party

"Are you sure your leg is better?" she said with a raised eyebrow as her husband tried to clamber up the hastily slapped-together footstool. His shaking was definitely not entirely due to the unsteadiness of his platform, but he waved her worries aside with the measuring tape he was holding. The eyebrow never lowered as her gaze shifted to their black-feathered friend in the corner, whose face she expected looked amused, though his smiles never seemed to reach his eyes. "That's certainly not what you told the commander when we got home yesterday, if I remember correctly," Nulaidutice stated coolly, but the accusation didn't need any bite to land.

Almost knocking over his support as he turned to face his wife, wobbling as he did, Lapiutalnice replied, "I may have fibbed a little bit, but honestly it felt worse then. Probably because we just finished a long day of travel."

"In a cart," his wife retorted as he tried to go back to taking measurements, the comment being met with a groan.

"Sitting that long is enough to make anyone's leg stiff. Besides, how am I supposed to finish this if I'm being rushed back to the Gaité for most of the month?" he retorted, getting rather annoyed at this point.

Seeing Lapiutalnice's mood deteriorating, she decided to drop the issue. "Would be quieter, at least," Nulaidutice teased as she stepped closer to help steady him at the machine. He had almost fallen in as he started trying to reach further parts for inspection. But getting the measurements needed to start planning further progress was the only thing on his brain, whatever that would look like.

"Certainly," Piqoug added with a yawn. "He's honestly so boring to visit at the Gaité, I still wonder how we became friends there. He's much more interesting at work, so I'm not gonna report him. That's the commander's problem, not mine, if soldier boy here would rather spend his time tinkering with his toy. Speaking of which, what exactly are we working on, again?"

"An engine," came the quick reply from the elf man, glad to change the subject back onto his project. "Without good wind we need this thing to be able to go thirty to forty knots on the ground before she can take off. Otherwise her weight will be too much and the lift won't carry it, at least that's what Nulai's math says."

"Still don't know how you tricked me into doing that," Nulaidutice rolled her eyes in response, but her husband ignored it and just continued talking.

"If we can get a propeller spinning fast enough on the front, we might be able to get it going that fast," he said as he finished his last stretch of the measuring tape.

"You'd have to maintain it too dear," his wife once again chimed in as she helped pull him back to the safety of solid ground. "Especially at it's weight, the stupid sky boat will lose speed rapidly once it loses momentum. You'll be gliding back to the ground once the propellant stops at best."

"Hence why you are so against the tension idea," he replied, the dark-winged harpy realizing this must have been most of their conversation on the way back home.

"I'll look at the amount of space you have," she said, though without much conviction, "I just doubt you'll be able to get a rope tense enough in that space to get it going at thirty knots, let alone keep it going at that speed for any amount of time."

"That thing must be heavy," Piqoug snorted as he looked upon the strange device, which was still damaged from its crash in the lake a few days earlier. "I'm glad I don't need to be going thirty knots for takeoff."

"That's because you can flap your wings to get lift, dear, imagine trying to take off by only running with your wings outstretched, on flat ground," Nulaidutice explained, causing the bird man to raise his own eyebrow toward the machine in response.

"On flat ground, even with flapping it's hard to get into the air," he concurred with the judgment. "That's why I always run off the barn roof when leaving here."

"Now you see why everyone thinks my husband is insane," she laughed, but Piqoug could almost hear some real anxiety hidden behind the sass this time. He wondered how long it would be before she snapped under the pressure she was probably facing.

"Oh, you didn't need to convince me," he replied, pointing a taloned hand to his chest. "I wouldn't talk to him so much if he was. No offense, Nulaidutice, but sane elves are rather stuffy and boring to talk to. He's like hanging around with humans, but without the mood swings."

"Well, I'm glad you like hanging out with the humans so much," she smirked as she clapped her husband on the back, "but around here, being like a human isn't very respectable."

"I've noticed," the bird man chuckled. "You elves seem almost allergic to fun."

Lapiutalnice, finally getting tired of the other two discussing him right in front of his face, stepped in to reply, "Well then, why don't you join us for tea? You can help us figure out how to build an engine strong enough to get this thing off the ground!"

Though he knew Lapiutalnice meant it in good faith, the harpy could not help but chuckle at the request, "Oh no, I'm no code-breaker, numbers aren't my thing. I am but a humble courier, and speaking of which, I should probably get back to my rounds."

"Shame," the elf man said, though there was a smile on his face, "but thank you for checking in anyway, Piqoug, hopefully you'll be back around by the time we test a real flight!"

"That does sound more interesting," the bird man admitted

before heading toward the ladder leading up to the barn roof. The elf couple followed suit, reaching the back door to their house just in time to watch their friend take his leap, his great black wings unfurled as he coasted on the breeze, rising higher and higher to the point where soaring would be effortless for him. Nulaidutice could tell it never ceased to fascinate her husband, as even while she was getting the tea started, he hadn't left the doorway, his eyes glued on the sky.

"Okay, doofus," she finally snorted, bringing a tray of peanut cakes to the table to complete their afternoon meal, "he's gotta be a tiny speck by now, and besides we need to get working on your stupid designs if we're going to finish them before dinner."

"So you are gonna help," the elf man replied, turning around with a smirk.

"If I don't now I've wasted my entire morning standing out there with you," she grunted as she unfurled a large roll of paper and her drafting tools. "Sunk cost fallacy has set in."

"Kind of like our marriage, huh," chuckled Lapiutalnice as he sat down across the table from her, grabbing one of the dozen peanut cakes before pouring the tea. He knew he had better take it now if he wanted any.

From across the table, though, his comment was simply met with a mumbling dismissal, "The damage is already done there, we're past the point of no return," before she went back to chewing the whole pastry she had shoved in her mouth. Taking her pencil in one hand and a second cake in the other, she began to cover the paper with numbers and diagrams which didn't make much sense to the elf man, though he tried his hardest to decipher her spidery elvish scrawl as she worked. He didn't need to read it to know the math wasn't going well, however, due both to the scowl on Nulaidutice's face and how she would down a single cup of tea in between her peanut sweets.

After he'd watched the sun go by for about ten minutes, his wife finally looked back up at him from across their little round table. "Isn't going to work," she said through a mouth-full of oat and peanut debris. "I didn't do the intense math, but just the preliminary equations suggest that we'd need an absurd amount of rope just for takeoff. Unless you think we can fit a mile of coil in under a few yards, I don't think we're going to get anywhere."

"Okay, rope doesn't work," Lapiutalnice said methodically, sitting back in his chair as he continued watching the clouds. "Are there other materials that would work better?"

"Well," his wife said after swallowing for once, "most civilian applications of tension utilize springs instead of rope, such as my mother's clock over there. When you wind it up it has a metal coil that tightens and slowly releases over time."

"That sounds like it'd be more compact," the elf man replied hopefully, but his wife was already shaking her head.

"For slow applications like the clock it works just fine," she said, though she was already doing math again to confirm her suspicions. "To generate enough energy to move your stupid sky boat I'm guessing we're either going to warp the metal under the pressure or require a far greater force to wind the bloody thing up. Possibly both. It also isn't helping that this needs to be a gradual release of energy rather than sudden for any of these things."

"So, what you're saying is metal is too rigid and rope isn't stretchy enough," her husband commented as he sipped his own tea methodically, thinking the problem over.

"Right," she confirmed slowly, "at least, that's the super over-simplified version of the problem. If we had something that was more elastic than rope which could be slung under the ship it would probably solve at least some of our problems."

"Rubber," was all that Lapiutalnice had to say to get his wife to glare at him.

"And where do you think we're going to find a mile of rubber coil?" she shot back, this time with a little less sarcasm and a little more worry.

"Would it take a mile?" he replied calmly. "If the rope takes that much, then wouldn't the rubber take less?"

Silently, not able to protest but also not being super happy at the prospect of potentially needing to locate large amounts of rubber in the near future, Nulaidutice went back to her work. This time it took far longer, with hours passing instead of minutes. As the sun continued its crawl across the sky, the elf man stopped watching it and began to clear and clean the dishes from their afternoon tea to prepare for the next meal.

Each time he came back from the well with a load of dishes, he'd still find her bent over the ever-growing number of papers she had placed in front of her, coated in math and diagrams. Some were crossed out, others erased, some circled or starred, but not much of it made much sense to the elf man. Her two decades of university, though not that long, had certainly helped her grasp physics better than himself. She was entirely wasted working on the Gaités.

It wasn't until the shadows had started to lengthen that Nulaidutice finally emerged from her work. She didn't say anything, but stretched out her tired arms and legs which were getting stiff from sitting so long. Leaning forward on the back of her chair, her husband surveyed the mess of notes in front of him, "Well, at least you had to think about it."

"Think a little too hard about it," she said with a tired voice as she slumped back forward. "Could you be a gent and grab me a tea, dear?"

Placing the whole bottle down in front of his wife, he pulled his chair to the other side of the table both to continue to try and read what his wife had worked out and give her something more comfortable to slouch on than the table. The feel of her wild hair was refreshing, but the math did not look nearly as much so. Most of it was crossed out, some of it scribbled rather aggressively as if in frustration, and what did seem to work looked less consequential than what didn't.

It also wasn't helping that Nulaidutice remained completely

silent as they sat in the growing twilight, simply looking out the windows and drinking large swaths of her beverage at a time. If it wasn't loaded with caffeine she might have fallen asleep right there and then. To be fair, he wouldn't have minded taking a nap himself – the gentle glow and dancing shadows in the house set the perfect mood for it.

He let the silence last a good while before he interrupted it, both elves looking out toward the distant peaks of the Brödbrutals across the steppe, barely visible over the rolling hills and farms, like jagged white teeth on the horizon. They were tinged red in the dusk, glowing brightly in the last rays of the day, a beautiful sight to take his mind off his daunting task. "I love those mountains," he whispered softly as he wrapped himself around his wife.

Lapiutalnice's comment was met with a face full of hair as his wife adjusted her slouch to look at him. As expected, a smirk had crossed her freckled cheeks once again as she prepared her snark, "How would you know? You've never been to them, dumbo."

"I can see them, can't I?" he laughed back as he returned to gazing out at them. "Though I certainly wouldn't mind going. The idea of being so far above the world sounds amazing to me."

"Who would have thought," she giggled as her eyes rolled. "From what I hear it's mostly a dry waste populated by warring pek strongholds, orcs, and beastfolk clans. Let the caravans come out to us, we have our own mountains we can visit sometime."

"Which are what?" Lapiutalnice had his own turn to laugh back. "Dry alpine forests filled with warring Dark Elf strongholds that caravans carrying gunpowder come rolling out of? So much different."

This got a snort and a grin out of his wife, "At least we don't have savage tribes of orcs and beastfolk wandering ours, just marauding armies of civilized elves."

"I've had enough of those for a lifetime," he chuckled in return. "I think I'll risk the minotaurs and gray folk. Maybe if I follow the caravans up into the mountains, we'll be able to settle in a pek mine before bumping into them."

"You'd go crazy in a pek mountain home," Nulaidutice laughed uncontrollably now. "They are almost entirely underground, you dingus! Where would you get your sky fix up there?"

"At least it wouldn't be boring," he replied calmly. "It wouldn't be the Gaité, where all we do is look intimidating to scare off orc clans, which learned generations ago that shields don't block bullets. While I'd rather the orcs keep their distance than fight them, I have no interest sitting around and pretending to do so either."

"It's okay, love," the elf woman spoke as she kissed her husband's cheek. "We'll make sure you don't die with the only thing you've done in your life having been sitting in a wooden box. However, I'm going to need the kitchen here in a bit, so we're going to have to stand up."

"And what is going on in the kitchen, exactly?" laughed Lapiutalnice as he helped his wife get her sleeping legs under her after having sat for several hours. It didn't take long for the blood to flow back into them, though, and for her to walk him toward the yard.

"Because I'm having some of the girls from work over tonight, they wanted to hear about your crash on the lake, and I wanted to brag about my husband for once. I don't need you to mess that up, so I'm kicking you out," she said, shoving him out the back door playfully. "Go and work on your project or something. Don't worry, I'll keep them occupied so you don't have to deal with the publicity yet, while it is still in my power to spare you at least. Besides, we'll probably end up talking about the technical details your manly butt does not have the education to keep up with."

"Like I didn't just spend the afternoon working on a physics problem with you," he winked and rolled his eyes as he readjusted his glasses. But she had correctly assessed his opinions on the situation, thus he began hobbling his way over toward the large dark object in the late twilight. His wife watched with her hands on her hips from the house to make sure he got to his hiding place all right, and soon after he had settled in the barn, he could hear the voices of the other women drifting from the lamplit windows, followed by the shut of the door behind her.

Sadly, he still did not know the results of that physics problem, so he was not sure exactly what to do to move the project forward. However, he did have plenty of repairs that could be done after the crash so he decided he could work on those instead. Gathering his tools, he began cutting out new wings and other protruding parts that had come off when he hit the water. The sun went down while he worked, and the chill of the night crept in, forcing the elf man to light a fire both for light and heat.

He would never have stopped if he hadn't run out of wood back in the barn – he must have been burning quite a bit in the forge over the past week. The elf man was going to have to break into the house's firewood supply, much to his disgruntlement. Lumber was slightly costly out on the plains, but Tivowichaisch wasn't that far to the south; he and Nulaidutice could take a couple day's ride to get some more cheap if they wanted to. He hobbled back out of the barn quietly, trying not to suddenly become the spotlight of the dinner party.

Keeping as quiet as he could, Lapiutalnice's rummaging beside the kitchen door accomplished an unintended goal: it also let him hear what they were saying. And what he heard made him pause a moment. It didn't sound like a cheerful meal at this point, though it was his wife's cooking. "Nulaidutice, this is a worrying pattern, and has got to stop," he heard one of the voices say with some level of forced concern. "You're doing it again, and this time you have no excuse, there is no gain in it. You said it yourself, it is impossible, the science doesn't check out. You aren't doing him any favors by doing this, you are just destroying your reputation and his chances at becoming a good soldier to serve this country in the only way a man can."

"Maybe what I do with my household is my own business,"

he then heard his wife snap back at her accuser, "and those prying need to learn to respect my privacy. We proved the concept worked in theory, I don't find it alarming in the slightest that we haven't found a way to make it work in practice with only one afternoon of trying. Besides, if he actually succeeds at this, he'll have done more good for not only this country but this world than most who came before him. It is a gamble I have calculated and decided to take, which is my right to do."

"It is also your right to say no," a much calmer voice drifted into the night air, which was eerily still compared to Lapiutalnice's pounding heartbeat. "It makes no sense to keep up this game. I know you find your husband's obsession cute, but those are the words of a much younger and less wise woman. I know you are smarter than this, you are already seeing where this is leading. Visits from the commander, his best friend being a harpy, no children at your age, what is going to wake you up to the fact that he is trouble Nulai?"

"Look, Nulaidutice," came a third voice into the assault, "if you insist on keeping this pet husband around, at least take another husband from the Gaité like I've suggested multiple times. Then at least some of the whispering might stop, even though you're keeping your insane one around. We work with you, dear, we know you are level-headed enough to see the value in this. To be frank, keeping him around in general is acting rather human for you, but I suppose we all have our ugly parts hidden underneath."

Over the chirping of the crickets, he could barely hear his wife's seething breaths, though she did not respond to these accusations. There was not much she could say – they were all right, as he himself knew far too well. He couldn't help but feel a little guilty as he absorbed just how much trouble he was causing her. She had always joked about not getting mixed up in the project, but now he was wondering if he should have actually kept her out of it. That was a little hard to do when she was married to him, and thus funding the project, but perhaps it would have mitigated it.

Drawing back some tears, he hoisted the firewood quietly and headed back to the barn, though he no longer planned on revitalizing the smoldering coals at this point. No, his thoughts were too confused to continue working. Like her, he had weighed the risks and thought this course of action was worth it, but he now could see it was more complicated than first calculated. He had just been sheltered under Nulaidutice's wing for too long to see it.

An hour or two passed in the chilly summer night as he listened to the crickets chirp their songs, doing nothing but look at the machine that was causing them so much trouble. He wondered if he was really just acting human in all this. Yes, he had known it was a gamble, one that now didn't seem to be paying off, but was he right in taking it? It was the nature of risk, after all. Yet, had that been wise, or logical, the elvish decision? Did it even matter?

He had just decided to light a lamp when he finally heard the footsteps from his wife stomping down from the house. Her muttering became audible even before her silhouette appeared in the doorway. He didn't need to see any more details than the sparse starlight permitted to tell that she was utterly distraught – the rest of the evening must have been as bad as the moment he had overheard.

It took a little while for the sounds of pounding feet to make their way across the barn, where they found Lapiutalnice contemplating his project. As his wife's figure started to appear in the lamplight, he turned from his work to speak to her, say some word of comfort and apologize for the trouble he had been giving her. But he wasn't able to get a single word out before he was wrapped in a hug so hard he almost lost his balance and knocked over his toolkit while steadying himself. The ringing clatter of it's spilled contents was quickly drowned out by the heaving sobs he shouldn't have been surprised to feel turning into cascading rivers running down his back.

"I..." he muttered quickly, trying to catch up with the sudden amount of emotion being poured out on him, "I'm sorry..." But he was never able to finish the sentence, and probably for the better, too. Nulaidutice was absolutely charged that evening, in a way he had never seen anyone else.

"We're building the bloody sky boat," she replied bluntly, annihilating her husband's expectations. "We're building it even if it kills us. When I get back home tomorrow I'm drafting as many takes on the engine as I can. It will fly."

"Nulai," he whispered softly, not sure how to feel. She was acting very human. "I overheard some of the conversation, and if the math doesn't work then you've done everything you can. At this point it really might be a mad dream, and if you don't want to risk crashing with me..." he tried to reply, but he was cut off by his wife's sobbing turning to rage.

Flinging him onto the ground with his tools, she stood back to her feet, growling not exactly toward her husband, but the entire barn (and likely the entire world beyond as well). "Do you think I only started taking that risk now?!" she bellowed into the air, stomping back and forth in the dim light. "You know full well I didn't! I took that risk the moment you set your heart on this project. And guess what? I don't regret it! Nothing they say can make me regret it, this is what why I married you in the first place!"

"Nulai," Lapiutalnice said hesitantly, quickly getting to a seated position to try to calm the fire welling up inside his wife, "you don't have to attach yourself to this. I'm going to fly or fall with this machine, but you can spare yourself from it. They didn't need to tell me it is a foolish dream, I know, but it's all I have, you risk far more than me."

"How, by divorcing you?" she glowered, leaning forward in the light of the lamp as she turned to face him. "Then what, pick up some toy soldier who will give me kids? Is that not the same trap you are trying to avoid in the Gaité? Am I not allowed to dream like you are?"

Lapiutalnice's cheeks flushed with embarrassment, it was his turn to feel high emotions. He really did not have a response to that. She was right, after all. If he had the right to chance it with Lady Luck, then his wife certainly did. But she had so much more on the line than him – he had already been an outcast before he started building the Lapudrum. A much smaller cost than the one his wife, the well respected engineer from the forest, was already paying.

Some of this confusion must have gotten past the shadows of his face, because the anger subsided rapidly in Nulaidutice's. "Come on," she finally said, face glittering with tears, "let's go to bed, Lapiu. We're both clearly far too emotional at the moment to be talking about important things. Tomorrow we can start working on some form of propellant, and thus making this bloody machine fly."

Seeing his opportunity to ease his own tensions as well as his wife's, Lapiutalnice quickly agreed to the prospect and offered his hand as they began the journey back toward the house. He left his tools out and scattered; he would just be taking them out again the next morning, and he wanted to get Nulaidutice to sleep as fast as he could. She seemed to have calmed down, though – as they walked under the starlit skies, the only hint of her earlier outburst was in her crushing grip. A vice that did not release him until the stars disappeared behind the ceiling of their home, and the sound of his wife's snoring began.

6 The Engine

"Do not let that thing slip!" Nulaidutice's sharp voice came out even a little harsh to herself. But with her face being right next to the thick rubber cord she was trying her darnedest to secure, she did not want a repeat of the last incident. She had enough on the line right now; she didn't need to put her face at risk too. Working underneath the machine, she could not see Lapiutalnice's reaction to her snap, she could only see where his twig-like arms were straining to hold the rubber coil taut. She didn't want all it's weight resting on the metal hook at the base of the tail, at least until she was finished connecting the mechanism to the propeller and safely out of the way if things broke again.

The strand of black material was still quivering from when her husband had shifted his weight, vibrating like a violin string with the vast amounts of potential energy in the coil. As she regained her composure she heard the elf man grunt in response to her alarm, "I know that one sounded bad, but the steel hook seems to be holding much better than the wooden beam. I don't think we're at risk of repeating the last attempt..."

But she cut off her husband's voice before he could continue, "I'm the one risking my face here, not you. I'll decide when you're allowed to stop helping that hook out." No muffled comment came from behind the canvas body of the device which she now worked on in peace. She reveled in those quiet few minutes; she was not in the mood to be bantering right now – she couldn't guarantee that any snide comment she made wouldn't be sincere.

The moment didn't last forever, though. Lapiutalnice seemed more insecure than usual, despite her not wanting to put up with it. "That would be a shame," he grunted as he tried to alleviate most of the pressure the band was asserting. "A raw mark would not suit your freckles well." Just with all his other meager attempts at flirting this morning, she ignored it. She wondered how many times she'd have to stonewall him before he got the hint.

She had woken up at the crack of dawn, but her "period length being abnormal" notice to the construction office was barely necessary – her lady friends would have made it clear she had other priorities right now. Mostly Nulaidutice had wanted to use the time to avoid those people she was in such a foul mood with and had gotten into the construction supplier and out with the rubber coil before anyone, besides the disgruntled warehouse manager, was there to judge her. Probably would have been a smoother conversation if she had slept better, but she had only reluctantly gone to bed the night before when her husband started making worried looks from across the room. He had been much quieter that day as she fought desperately with physics to make this stupid coil engine work without rest. It seemed even the laws of reality were trying to make her look crazy.

But with a final bolt squeezed into place, her act of defiance against the logical order of the universe was finished. With the propeller safely attached to the rubber coil she rolled out from under the machine. "You can let it sit now," she said tersely as she brushed straw from her work dress, already looking for the crank she would use to wind up the device. From the corner of her eye, she could see her husband exchange a look with an equally tense barn cat standing on top of the Lapudrum, but he also didn't protest being released from his duty. With a hardy slap she heard the taut rubber snap into place, and she tilted a pointed ear toward the device. It groaned as it strained under the pressure, but this time it held strong – the metal hook had done it's job as her husband had thought it would. "Good," the elf woman grunted as she moved toward the next task. "Now we need to make sure it doesn't tear the thing apart when we wind it up."

She was already stooping to grab the crank when all her momentum was stopped in its tracks by her husband's voice. "I think we should take a break dear," he said simply. She could hear him stumbling to his feet, using the machine as a crutch to get off the floor and face her. He was speaking calmly, but this time she could hear a stern seriousness in his voice. This required her to take a moment to collect herself before she said something she regretted, but this man had some audacity to talk to his wife in such a tone. It took a second for her to remember that is part of why she had married him in the first place, but right now it wasn't helping get the job done. The job that he had started, she noted angrily to herself.

"Lapiutalnice," she said in a cold, even, tone, both trying to remind him who was in charge and appeal to his logic, "that cord is taut right now, if we leave it until later it will probably have warped the whole machine, and then we will have to restart." It was a mystery to her what this man was even thinking. He had her full support and attention for his stupid project now, couldn't he just be grateful and accept the help? He needed her for this anyway, he might have had the imagination to dream up this thing, but it was her who spent all of the previous day trying to make that dream a reality. It was her who had worked through the heat of the day to find a solution to the impossible problem, it was her who had to clean up after her husband's ambitions. The least he could do was not get in the way while she was doing it, though some cooperation would have been appreciated.

But he clearly had no plans to back down this time, and actually shocked the elf woman by swiftly dismantling the logic she had thrown at him. "We can pull it off for now," her husband replied firmly. "You got it secured at the front, it should be relatively easy to pull on and off at this point. The Lapudrum isn't going anywhere, dear, we can test it after a break. I'm thinking some breakfast sounds good." Nulaidutice's mind raced as she tried to justify her emotions, but unfortunately he was right. They needed to eat at some point, and now was as good a time as any, but she did not want to. She vehemently did not want to, and that vehemence is what finally caught her off guard. He was right, taking a break only made sense, and yet the burning drive was not leaving her – she could not agree to it. She hadn't stopped since the tea party a few nights ago, and she knew she was going to burn herself out if she kept this up. But she couldn't, she had to keep going, and suddenly the thought struck her: is this what humans felt like all the time? It seemed like such an exhausting existence, and yet here she was.

"Here, let's compromise, then," he replied to her unstated argument. "Let's take a seat by the cats and just let our arms and legs ease up a bit. We'll get back to it before any harm is done." This was again such an elegant solution, and he probably needed to rest his arms after straining against the rubber for so long. Yet she hated the idea. She needed to keep going, but why, what would that accomplish? He was right, the stupid machine wasn't going anywhere, no one was coming to look for them, they could afford to pause, to sit for a second. Frustrated, the elf woman stalked her way over to the hay bale and sat herself a little more dramatically than intended. She could see the hint of a smile forming as her husband adjusted his glasses and shuffled over toward the spot himself, but he was wiser than to let it finish. Yet it was that very smirk that had caught her attention to begin with, told her of the personality in that man beyond just another soldier in the Gaité. Why was it so frustrating to her now?

As Lapiutalnice joined her he said nothing, and simply started petting the barn cat she had startled from his nap in the suddenness of her arrival. She could tell he was trying to appear at ease, to release the tensions of the situation, but she could not calm down. Her eyes never went to him, they were consumed by the device they were gazing upon, their fool's errand. Oh, how she hated the thing, even while she was filled with nothing but a desire to finish it. The boat-like canvas frame with the broad wings stored in the shadows of the barn behind it sat there, taunting her. It was so simple a concept, it was just like the kites her husband was so obsessed with, yet it sat just outside the realm of possibility. Tantalizingly within reach, and yet nothing she did could make the numbers really work.

As of now, she thought she had gotten the engine strong enough to take off and fly for a minute or two, but that would not be enough. She would need more than that to justify her actions, to justify her husband's dream. While a machine that could take off with a passenger was impressive, it still was not practical, still not worth pursuing. An idea that should have been abandoned in the conceptual stage. But she was so close, and if she could almost achieve it, then... then...

It was in the middle of this turmoil that the elf man leaning against her finally spoke again, and his words sent a chill through her spine, "Nulai, what are you trying to prove?"

Trying to prove his stupid dream right, that he wasn't a delusional menace to society, what else did the idiot think she was trying to prove? Yet that answer did not sit well with her even as it entered her head, and she knew it was wrong. If she was trying to prove that, then why was it affecting her so personally, why was she so angry? To an extent it was about that, but that was already a losing battle. The fact was the ladies were absolutely right – her husband was not acting logically and doing a whole lot more than flirting with Lady Luck at this point.

At the tea party, they hadn't been excited because they thought he might have been sane after all. No, they were excited that his wife's gamble may have been paying off despite his insanity. The ladies had hoped that the Fienlapus had proven the impossible over the lake, and their support vanished when the truth was revealed. Vanished when they saw how much more luck was needed, and how her husband's delusions were rubbing off on Nulaidutice herself. They had always told her that this man was trouble, that he was such a poor choice for a husband. Men with dreams were a problem – they destabilized their precarious balancing act the Failatgie Empire had formed to survive – but she could not abide in that logic.

She could not put up with a husband that existed purely as a play thing to give her kids until he died in some frontier skirmish and she got another one. It seemed boring, and if she wanted kids she could just attend the Gaité parties with the other young ladies. Sure it wasn't as respectable, but why was that so much better than actually marrying to have an interesting partner, why was it so much more foolish to find someone who could share in a dream? As she gazed upon the monument of foolishness sitting just beyond the rays of sunlight, she knew the ladies were right. She had made a mistake.

At least from their perspective she had. All this was doing was dragging down her career, dragging her attention away from her work, which was some of the most important in the empire. Most women would kill to be in her position, but then why did she keep choosing this, why did she keep looking forward to coming home to this problem of a man every night? Why was her logic and that of her people so opposed, wasn't logic objective? Why was her right answer so different from that of Failatgie's?

Finally, her pause for reflection did its work. She couldn't take the confusion any longer. She had subconsciously known this would happen if she diverted her focus from the task at hand. But there was no stopping it now, and all the frustration that had been burning inside of her fizzled out, leaving smoldering ashes of disoriented sadness. "I don't know," she finally sobbed as the emotional steeling she had done broke down on her. Tears of anger, doubt, and resentment all began to flow as Lapiutalnice closed in around her and the vision of the accursed project was blocked by the tangles of his rich brown hair. His soft brown hair, and gentle touch, reminding her exactly why she had gotten herself into this problem to begin with. She returned the embrace and pulled him in tight, feeling both the warmth of the morning sun and the elf man's body did not help settle the confusion in the slightest, but did stabilize her mind enough to acknowledge it. Why was she being shamed for this? Why was this man's eccentricity such a crime that it covered any rational reason to marry such a sympathetic person?

Together they sat in the growing sunlight as it climbed to its zenith. They remained still awhile, her husband occasionally picking bits of straw out of her hair as he waited for her mind to become coherent enough to reply to the question which had started this period of reflection. He was smart enough to see further prodding was necessary, and thus summed up her thoughts to her with shocking accuracy, "Is this for me or yourself? You know I don't need you to prove this works for me. I am well aware this is a dream, and I may sink rather than sail with it. I just also have nothing to lose, if it doesn't work I'll still be stuck in the military and thought of as a fool. But both those things were true before I started this journey. For you this is a true gamble, one I'm glad you've been so willing to take with me, but I think it's time we asked why."

"You're not going to get me to stop," she said hoarsely, burying her face into his shirt to avoid looking at the outside world. He had been paying much more attention than she thought he had, or maybe was just wiser than she gave him credit for.

"And I won't try to," he said calmly as he picked pieces of straw out of her hair. "Even if you don't have a rational reason to continue I will not stop you. I won't risk your rationality, then you might realize how bad of an idea marrying me was!" This comment caused her to flinch internally, and finally the pieces came together in a coherent way. They had both made that jest a hundred times, but they both knew it wasn't true. Even now she thought Lapiutalnice was likely joking, but it was time for her to actually take this accusation seriously for once.

"I think it was a logical decision," the elf woman whispered with full sincerity, finally saying what had been left implied their whole marriage. "I didn't want a husband who would spend all his time at the Gaité, what is the point of having a husband then? I might as well just mask up and hit the parties at that point. You're one of the few men I've met who had dreams, and was it wrong of me to enjoy that? The only reason this is even causing me problems is because Failatgie doesn't want that kind of logic, she wants me to want what she wants. But if I can prove this bloody boat of yours can fly, then maybe the empress and Paipadaívaen will want my logic, and then the ladies won't be able to accuse me any longer."

"This is true," she could feel him reply slowly, mulling over her reasoning. "However that is a shaky relationship you are trying to form with Failatgie. You're still at odds with the City of a Thousand Trees, she simply conceded ground here because you proved your point. The empire will continue pressing you from elsewhere, still trying to get you to mold into the image she wants. The Lapudrum just will become a part of that mold now, a part of the image they will want of you."

"Then what am I supposed to do?" Nulaidutice sighed as she leaned back to look out the windows into the brilliant sunlight, watching the dust caught in its rays drift softly by. "How do I stop making Failatgie my enemy and make her my ally?"

"You know I don't know, dear," the elf woman was surprised to hear her husband reply with equal anguish. "If I did I wouldn't be a soldier, would I?" She didn't really have anything to say back, but it did confirm what she was feeling inside. No matter what the ladies she worked with said, or what the empire wanted her to do, she had made the most logical decision of her life when she married this man. She might be acting human at this moment, but she had been acting like a true elf then. Thus, she rested in the security of that knowledge until the rays of the morning sun left them in the shade of the barn, alone with the Lapudrum that had been causing them so much trouble.

Eventually as the time wore on well past the handful of minutes they had been meaning to sit there, Nulaidutice turned her head toward the vessel waiting in the shade. It seemed so much less threatening now, as if she'd made a truce with the machine. It was never the problem, though it had taken her awhile to realize it. It was not the source of her troubles, just a symptom of it, and even if she addressed that symptom, it would change nothing. And she was starting to realize she was becoming okay with that.

But it had been a long time, and that rubber coil had to be hard to install for a reason, "We probably should actually test the propeller if we're going to do it today." Though it was wise, she lacked the conviction she had held earlier. Her husband had been right, it wasn't going anywhere, and all the hours she had been working without rest were starting to catch up to her as they sat in an ever-growing pile of barn cats, who were enjoying the lack of noise for a change.

Almost as if he had been waiting for this response, her husband jumped to his feet and took his wife's hand to raise her off the hay bale. "Help me take the coil off the back then, we'll test her later," he replied quickly. "Let's not risk our hopes drowning in our rationality quite yet. Instead let's get an even less wise decision to bury our logic in before reality grounds us again."

"And what would that be?" Nulaidutice asked with a raised eyebrow, a bit of a smirk starting to form on her lips as she prepared herself for whatever antics her husband was about to suggest. Taking his hand in gesture, though using her other to lift herself from the bale so as not to further damage the excited man's leg, she joined her husband as they hobbled their way over to their project.

"I say lets go to the parlor," he said with a grin. "Reason may be strong, but frozen desserts defeat it every time. You can't tell me we store all that ice for the good of the country or something. We have been beguiled by ice cream's taste ever since the dwarves taught us how to make it."

"I suppose you're right," the elf woman laughed as she helped her husband stoop down so they could dismantle the engine, "Don't tell the empress then, or she might try to ban parlors!" After they struggled to pull the rubber coil from the hook it had been set on, Nulaidutice did a quick inspection of the machine to make sure it hadn't received any damage in the time it had been under strain. Deeming the Lapudrum in good repair, she once again offered her support to her husband and the two started their walk out of the barn. It was not a short ride to the only parlor in Natniln, but that didn't matter right now. Their dream wasn't going anywhere, nor was her determination to see it through. This is what she had signed up for, and if the ladies could not see why she stayed then it was they who were the fools, not her.

7 The Flight

"They found us," groaned the elf man as he looked toward the crowd slowly trickling down the dusty roads. Women with their white broad-brimmed hats and colorful dresses, field workers sordidly dressed in only their dirty undershirts and pants, and even soldiers in beige and blue uniforms with guns casually slung over their shoulders. Waves and waves of them were coming, wandering toward the source of their amusement for the morning.

"How did they know," came his wife's scathing voice from where she was leaning on the Lapudrum, helping her husband get strapped into the device for its second test flight. Together the Fienlapus and Piqoug had just managed to crank the engine into place, the rubber coil running the length of the plane wound to the point of snapping below. Everything was ready for takeoff.

They thought they had done it quick enough to get their test in before others caught on, but it was almost as if the crowd had known. The whole town was showing up on cue for the main event. Even with his tinted goggles and flight helmet on, the disappointment was visible on Lapiutalnice's face. His wife's, however, held much fiercer emotions.

"It was probably the farm hands again, word spreads when you're bored," the harpy suggested from the other side of the device, his face showing much less emotion than the other two, but he put no effort into hiding the annoyance in his voice.

"I doubt it," Nulaidutice growled as she began tightening the straps holding her husband in, so aggressively he had to intervene to tell her they were tight enough.

"I do need to breathe, dear," he smiled sadly again as he took hold of his wife's hands.

She took no notice of the quip though, and instead was glaring with a burning rage out at the sea of uninvited guests. "They're here, the gossiping traitors."

"Nulai," the elf man sighed, "we don't know that it was them. They might not agree with your life decisions, but they didn't want to embarrass you either. In fact they seem to be trying very hard to protect your reputation."

"And what better way to get me to turn back than to pressure me to back down?" she snarled in reply to their defense. "I won't be converted to reason by reason, so then I need to be converted by pressure. They know full well why I haven't shown up to work this week, they must have been watching for this moment." Despite being well and done with the preparations at this point she had not descended from the side of the flying machine. She would make sure all those three's accusations were true, and more, no longer simply tolerating this project but actively participating in it.

"Well," Lapiutalnice spoke softly, "you'd think they'd realize it's a little late for that now. They seem to underestimate the fire they lit inside you. A flame that has caused you much trouble, but I'm glad you graced me with it regardless I wouldn't be here without your help."

This finally brought a smile back to her face, a small half-smile, but a smile nonetheless. Turning her face back from the crowd, she finally met her husband's gaze again, and the crowd disappeared for the moment. It was just them, their sole loyal friend, and the Lapudrum, getting ready to chance it with Lady Luck another time. "You would have found a way. You always do. I am just lucky to have been the one who decided to chance it with you."

"The crowd is getting close," Piqoug stated urgently. "If we wait much longer they might start blocking our takeoff." Sure enough, the voices of the crowd were becoming audible, their excited drone carried on the wind toward them, the same wind that would hopefully carry their mad dream to the clouds.

"Then we better get flying," Nulaidutice smugly replied, a smirk finally filling up the whole of her lips. "Show the world what you can do, Lapiu, show the empire what she has lost because she wasn't willing to flirt with Lady Luck like you." Then to seal her own fate with him, she leaned as far into the cockpit as she could and caught her husband in a passionate and obvious kiss for luck. With that she hopped off the side of the machine, leaving Lapiutalnice alone at the helm of his sky boat, ready to soar off into the sky.

"You got this, brother," the black-winged harpy called, reaching up from the side. "I'm excited to switch places and watch you from the ground for a change. Me and Nulaidutice will do what we can to hold the crowd off so you can land." Gloved and taloned hands met in a grasp of solidarity for a moment, just long enough to give a warm smile to match, one that conveyed all the gratitude for the best friend's support, as well.

Then Lapiutalnice turned his head toward the field in front of him, and the rest of the reality disappeared. The long stretch of land just had the drying hay bundled off of it, leaving the field open from the tall grass of the steppe and traffic alike. The only place nearby which had enough space to get up to fifty knots on flat enough ground. Far, far down at the end of his narrow world, he could see the trees forming a wind-block, the tall cottonwoods looking like shrubs in the distance. These were the fence he'd need to clear, and for once he had the confidence that it could be done.

Putting his hand on the lever which would disengage the lock on the propeller, he took a deep breath. Raising his eyes up to the clouds which he had always wanted to join, he let the beautiful feeling wash over him. This was it, time to see if his machine would fly. It was then that the noise of the crowd started to break into his small bubble of reality, and he knew if he wanted a clear runway, he couldn't wait any longer. Thus, he cranked down the switch and the roar of the propeller coming to life drowned out the mob which he rapidly began to leave behind.

The wheels sped over the dry dirt ground, kicking up the dust under the grass as it did. He could never have known just how fast fifty knots was until he began approaching speed, and noticed those trees at the end of the field were approaching much faster than he had thought possible. They looked like a rushing line of soldiers, barreling toward him to prevent him from leaving the ground. As formidable as the hewn timber walls of the Gaité, trying to remind the fool that reality had laws which he must obey.

Though afraid, he hadn't quite built up enough speed – he knew he didn't have time left to clear the looming wall if he didn't act. So, without further hesitation, he pulled the stick back, and the flaps on the wings moved up in response. Much to his own amazement, the sky boat responded in kind, and its tight hold on the ground loosened as it began to turn upwards toward the sky. Pulling back harder, soon he lost all sight of the approaching cottonwoods and any other hint of the world below. All that he could see was the Lapudrum's spinning propeller and the glittering morning sun gazing down upon him from between the clouds.

He had done it – he was flying!

The revelation sank in all at once as he looked out into the blue and then over the side of his vessel. Down below to his left were the wide rolling lands of the steppe before they turned into mountains far away, and to his right the tall maples and oaks of Tivowichaisch as Daechûg turned into the forests from which the elves came. From this high up it was hard to see the village he lived in, as it was mostly blocked by the boat in which he rode. The homes and farms of those who ridiculed him blocked out by canvas wings, and their cries by the roaring wind on which he flew. He had won, it had worked! He could be called a fool no longer.

He wished he never had to confront the crowd though; he did not need their recognition. He simply had wanted to fly, and now his wish was granted. All that would come after hitting the ground again could wait until he was there. For now those worries were far below him, swallowed up by the clear blue sky. Yet end it had to; his coil would not last forever, or even that much longer according to his wife's words, so as quickly as he had left the field he was turning back toward it. The image of the infinite blue replaced with the coarse brown grass and dry leaves of the world below. And beyond the crowd of shocked onlookers ready to receive the one they had taunted and proven them wrong. The one who had flown.

But even as he was banking, he could see Lady Luck's face turning from him. It looked an awful lot like a propeller that had ceased to spin, the engine becoming fully uncoiled. He had built all the speed he would be getting for this flight. He wasn't alarmed yet, he was pulling the machine back to being level and heading into a descent now, that should be enough to keep him gliding to safety. Yet what he nor his wife hadn't accounted for was that the propeller's mischief was not over, as the rubber coil had unwound itself at such speed that it began recoiling in the opposite direction. This worked in Lapiutalnice's advantage for a few seconds until the momentum ran out, and it began to unravel again, spinning the propeller backwards

Attempting to push against the vessel instead of with it now, the disruption was enough to cause the Lapudrum to shake and veer from its course. Its pilot gripped the stick as hard as he could and tried to keep the machine from flipping over and spinning out, but it was no use. Far worse even than it spinning on the descent, the counter-force began turning the nose of the device away from the earth, back up into the air. Past that point there was no salvaging the situation, and Lapiutalnice found himself barreling toward the hard sun-baked earth below. One minute he'd see the sky and glare of the sun, the next the dull earth and colorful crowd, scattering as the meteor approached its point of impact. Finally he realized all he could do was accept his fate, and hunkered low into the machine, hoping that would help him keep his head on impact. It was the only hope he had.

The impact was surprisingly less terrifying than the descent: with the crack of wood and spray of dirt the anticipation was over. All around him the Lapudrum came undone as it hit the ground at high speed, shattering like a bullet upon the earth, and then it was done. Almost as suddenly as he had hit the ground, his memory blacked out, and all that filled his mind was the vision of the clouds and the sound of the wind. Not as dreams as they had been his whole life, but now as memories. He had flown.

—◦◦◦—

"LAPIU!" the barely audible voice of his wife came through the ringing in his ears and throbbing head. Dazed, he looked up to see the silhouette of her form surrounded by radiant rays of the sun, like a brilliant star reaching into the crumpled craft. Delicate fingers grasped at his shirt and began dragging him out of his canvas grave into that beautiful light. As he was pulled from what remained of the Lapudrum, the ethereal near-death experience began to fade back into reality.

As his head cleared, the elf man began to see just how bad the situation was, and he was truly lucky to be alive. He had hit the ground fast and at an angle, causing the whole craft to skid and roll sideways. A row of dirt like a plow line marked where the machine had smashed into the earth and began sliding, only broken up in the places where it had bounced as it flipped on its side.

The Lapudrum itself was in such a condition that he wondered how he had survived. The canvas wings had been wrapped up around the battered body like a blanket, the propeller missing several blades and the rubber coil snapped. Lady Luck must really enjoy his company to bring him through all of that. But not so for

Lapiutalnice's life work, there was no way to recover the corpse of a machine that his wife was pulling him out of.

It had just been a test, though; he had known it would not come out perfect. They would be able to avoid these problems in the future with the lessons learned, and probably should also make a device to allow him to escape the vessel before it fell from the sky this time. Safety measures were unfortunately usually thought of after the disaster, not before, but they wouldn't be needed again. Next time he would be able to land, he could feel it.

He was about to bring his thoughts up with his wife until he was laid down in the grass next to the wreckage. With his head resting on her lap, he finally was able to get a good look at her face, and the tears streaking down her face stopped him in his tracks. The distress was obvious, and then he remembered he had almost died. He still might, even, as his vision was still blurred, his ears still ringing, and his head, how his head hurt. The only thing keeping him from fading to black was the warm salty rain that fell on him, reminding him of his duties to life.

Soon another dark figure joined her, as the feathery head of Piqoug knelt beside the two and started pulling and prodding at his friend, grasping and feeling around for anything broken or not moving properly. Eventually he concluded, "His leg has re-broken, and judging by how dazed he looks he likely has a concussion. But I've seen much worse from failed landings. He should recover, Nulai, don't worry." Then leaning in so close his lips almost touched Lapiutalnice's face he said, "Can you hear me buddy? You had quite the nasty fall for your second landing."

"I don't seem to be very good at them," admitted the elf man hoarsely, his senses beginning to return to him.

This got the bird man's eyes to light up warmly as he patted his friend's shoulder. "It takes us years to get good at it, that'll come in time, as long as you don't kill yourself trying first," the black bird chuckled in response, helping Nulaidutice bring him from laying down to a seated position, leaning against his friend for support. Glad to hear the encouragement, Lapiutalnice's first response to seeing the crowd which had gathered around him was to smile a dazed little smile, thinking they must have been as excited as he was with the way things had turned out. It wasn't until the ringing in his ears began clearing that he realized the crowd was not cheering but jeering.

"So much for elves flying, as they already knew," he heard one voice say, followed closely by another. "What a reckless stunt to prove their machine can go up into the sky but can't come back down!" Now he understood why his wife had remained silent as the tears streaked off her face and soaked his shirt. It wasn't just that he had almost died, which he expected she could handle now that he was recovering. It was the crowd's persistent disdain, and the tightening clench on his hand was an equally bad sign.

To his surprise it wasn't her but Piqoug that came to his defense first. "How blind are you? You can't even see wonder when it nearly kills you falling out of the sky," his crowing voice sounded viscous, causing the closer jeerers to back off. "So scared of risk that you only focus on the failure and forget the success. Do I have to remind you that this man FLEW! He did what none of the rest of you would do, because you said it was impossible, illogical. Take defeat graciously, or are you going to take the human folly and turn to bitterness instead?"

"Silence, bird!" one of the older ladies in the audience snarled back, clearly taking great offense at his remark like the feathered man had hoped. "I have been alive twice as long as you will live! I know a waste of time when I see it. Their machine was skirting the edge of physics as it is. They risked what they already knew the data was warning against and made a fool of themselves, it would have been better if they had done what the math told them!"

"Elves," the black-winged harpy literally spat onto the ground beside him. "You wonder why humans live their short lives in joy while you spend your centuries in misery. As far as I'm concerned this man here has lived more in the last few minutes than you will have in your entire life."

The rage was clear in the audience at this remark, angry shouts and slurs following, but Piqoug merely sat smugly, knowing that he was right. He had successfully gotten these elves to act very human. An achievement he would brag with Lapiutalnice about the for rest of his life. But in that accursed moment there were more accusations to be made.

"Nulaidutice," came a voice from the crowd, though the crying woman did not lift her head to meet it, "you knew this would happen. We talked about it not even a week ago! You knew the numbers didn't add up, the fact that it even got off the ground was the grace of Lady Luck washing over you. You've had your fun, now call your husband off, he's no use to the Gaité if he keeps hurting himself like this."

At the last remark the elf woman finally lifted her face from her husband's shoulder, and for the first time in the exchange Lapiutalnice was afraid. There was a fire in those eyes, a burning intensity he worried would not be satisfied without a fight. "He's not going back to the Gaité," was her one statement on the matter, and the finality of the remark was enough to shock most of the crowd into muttering.

"You stubborn woman!" growled a second voice. "I thought you were more reasonable than this! You know we need every man we can get at the borders, we don't breed like rats. Unlike the orcs, who might I remind you, have almost wiped out our kind before. We can't start a trend in the empire of wives keeping their husbands from war, we will die!"

"Then maybe I'll take him out of the empire's jurisdiction," she shouted back, standing to her feet as she did. "If you can't recognize the gift you received from my husband I'll bring him to someone who does. If you don't want him Piqoug makes it sound like the humans actually would, maybe we'll go to them."

"Muyítselt'e is a lovely region," the bird man interjected, partially to calm the elf woman down and partially to show solidarity.

"It's a little hot, but just across the ocean, any Sea Elf merchanting vessel can bring you there without issue."

"You would abandon us for the barbarians?" came the gasp from one of her coworkers. "Just because we're talking sense and you don't want to hear it!"

"I saw the Lapudrum fly today," snarled Nulaidutice, jabbing a finger into the other elf woman's chest. "I think it's you who aren't seeing reason. I always thought that we were the logical, the wise, great in learning and years. But you all are making me embarrassed to be an elf!"

"Nulai," suddenly came a soft voice from behind, as she whipped around to see her husband being helped toward her by the black-feathered man, "It's okay. The results are in, and we both knew it was skirting the edge of physics as it was. Even if we can get it to land, it will not fly long enough to be useful. Maybe one day we'll come up with an engine, but perhaps it is time we accept that it probably can't be done with our current technology. We know it is true as much as they do, even if they didn't have faith to try."

"They don't know you," she sobbed, clutching him so close all he could see was her pale hair. "I know we can figure this out. Maybe adding a larger coil will work, maybe I'm wrong. We can try it, at least then we'd know."

"Nulai," he whispered, though inwardly as distraught as his wife, "it is okay, it is over. You wouldn't have said what you did if it were not true. Like you always said but never meant, it is utterly impossible. All we would be doing is risking my life further to confirm what we already knew. It was a crazy dream, and we demonstrated so much. It's time for me to be the good husband you should have had from the beginning."

In response, he was finally released from the brutal embrace, faced with eyes filled with such genuine anger that he was relieved once he realized it was not directed at him. "What's a good husband good for?" she growled so loud the gathered women recoiled as she slandered herself. "If I had married to have kids, I would not have taken the one man in the Gaité who constantly stayed around. You were never a good husband, nor did I want you to be. I wanted a husband who I could share a dream with, no matter how far your head is up in the clouds when you made it. I didn't go to university for two decades to find a husband who only knew how to shoot and clean a gun, I wanted someone who could match me, and one day possibly even overtake me."

"Then I'm sorry I couldn't do that for you," Lapiutalnice replied quietly, well aware of the crowd muttering in the background. Letting Piqoug leave him to shaky legs, he reached forward and took Nulaidutice's hands in his own, still rough from her help in the construction of his crashed dreams, the pieces of which were lying fractured in the grass behind him. "But, I am grateful you let me try. To that I owe you the rebuilding of your reputation at the very least. Then once that is accomplished maybe we could move back to the sea, where the stories that took place out on the steppe can haunt you no longer."

"Idiot," she choked, though she was no longer shouting, "I don't care what the girls are saying. I don't care if I'm acting human, if this is what the humans are like then they are far more reasonable than us. I'm angry, I'm disappointed, and yes, I'm even surprised! But I don't want to forget this, the risk we took here is us, not you being off on soldier duties while I raise my heirs."

Pausing a moment to catch her breath, she finally seemed to calm down a bit. Turning her face and the ugly tears from her husband and the disapproving faces of the crowd, she looked toward the empty dirt road that eventually led down to their farm. The farm where they had spent so long building and planning, hoping beyond a hope in the machine that now lay in a heap behind them. Pulling Lapiutalnice in close, she rested her head against him as he turned to gaze with her. After a moment of silence she whispered, "I can see why you wanted to wait now. It really is a beautiful dream."

"An improbable one," Lapiutalnice replied, but his cynicism was only met with a squeezing sensation in his hands.

"But a beautiful one," Nulaidutice restated, closing her eyes and remaining still for her husband to lean on. Once again the elf man wondered what he had done for Lady Luck to smile on him so boldly.

Perhaps it was because, unlike those standing before him, he had been willing to roll the dice. He had trusted she would supply where others had deemed the risk too great, and maybe they were right. Maybe it didn't fly, not for long at least, maybe it never would, but he had tried, and that was enough. He took the risk and reaped a greater reward than he ever thought possible. Not a very elven way to do things, but why did he care? It worked, the proof was standing before him even as he heard the hoof beats coming down the lane.

Into view the dust cloud came, getting larger and larger as riders approached. The two watched in silence as the cavalry closed in, though it was rather surprising to see the blue uniforms of the imperial officers and not the beige of the frontier troops. At the lead of the column was a man Lapiutalnice did not deal with often, but definitely knew by sight. With a sharper face than most and large tricorn cap, the commander of the battalion was an obvious character. He wore his rank clearly, as it was likely all he had to his name, Lapiutalnice thought to himself. A man who embraced his destiny rather than resisted it. How different their lives had been.

Upon arrival the horses stopped not near him and his wife, but the wreckage of the Lapudrum. The commander did not dismount, but merely stared silently at the mangled heap of canvas, wood, and metal, choked in a snapped rubber coil. His expression stern and unreadable, he made no attempt to convey his purpose there. But Lapiutalnice did not need to guess at his purpose, it was as obvious as his rank. If it had shown promise, of course they would have been interested. Just as he had suspected.

He was beginning to be glad it had failed, and now he would not have to tempt that nightmare which crept along with the dream. It was over.

As if to confirm the thought, the commander turned his head to look at his underling, addressing him with a curt nod. "Trying to keep yourself injured longer I see soldier," he snorted, though Lapiutalnice suspected there was supposed to be some sarcasm in the statement.

"Unfortunately, the main thing broken in that attempt was my dreams, commander," he replied, though his leg would definitely need attention again. "There isn't a coil strong enough, rubber or otherwise, to power the rotor for long. This test confirmed her math rather than telling us something new."

"Yet," the commander said in a startling remark as he moved his attention to Nulaidutice, "if there was something that could power the rotor aside from tension the machine would fly?" His question was blunt and practical, making it all the more suspicious to the elf man.

Gripping his wife tighter he felt the elf woman take in a deep breath, "If there was some other way to create potential energy then yes, it would fly. It's basically a kite using momentum to stay airborne instead of wind, and seemed to have done well until the energy stored in the coil ran out."

"It certainly worked, if not a bit jerky," Lapiutalnice agreed hesitantly, eyeing the commander suspiciously but not wanting to lie to him. "I would have even been able to attempt a landing if the propeller hadn't reversed, causing the Lapudrum to stall midair. The engine seems to be the main problem that can't be overcome"

"Then come," the commander said, gesturing to two horses whose riders moved back in their saddles to admit extra passengers. The crowd of women's muttering became an uproar, demanding to know the meaning of it all, but the commander would not give them any word or let them approach, merely commenting, "For now this concerns only the Fienlapus and your empress. Know in good time she may choose to reveal her motives to you." Seeing little other choice the elf couple waved goodbye to Piqoug, who promised to meet them after their audience was over.

Once firmly seated he ordered the cavalry to a gallop, and they began thundering down the dirt roads once again. Farmland flew by, trees, bridges, and barns all flashing past as they rode. But above, the clouds remained constant, drifting along their lazy way, playing with the brilliant rays of sun. Again Lapiutalnice caught himself watching it, the anchor of his life, where his dreams always returned. Whether nightmares or fantasies worth living he was about to find out.

Racing the clouds above, they reached the Gaité. It's imposing rough wooden walls made it visible for miles around, the entire land between it and the next one on the frontier visible from its watchtowers. The formidable structure was able to see a wandering orc clan long before it was in striking range. Today though all they saw was the dust from their commander's hooves, the doors already having been thrust wide open to greet his arrival, the horses only slowing once inside the fort itself. Beige-uniformed infantrymen were busying themselves with cleaning cannons and muskets but shot suspicious glances at them, especially after they had dismounted and the imperial officer led the couple straight for the dugout basement of the facility. Then, naturally, he locked the door behind them all.

In the dusty candlelit gloom, the commander muttered in a quiet tone, "Her majesty does not wish this secret being revealed to our Teulyakeon rivals before it has to be. You will be held in court for high treason if you leak any information given to you down here. If it were not for the results of your flight today, I would have deemed neither of you worthy of this knowledge, but its relative success has changed things, and unfortunately there was no way around it." After making it clear how serious this all was, he gestured for them and his personal guard to follow him into the stuffy, dirt-walled room. Blue-coated soldiers posted themselves at the entrance of the room, both inside and out, as they stepped into the darkness. Soon they found themselves with another door between them and the sky above.

The only thing in that room was an old rickety table attended by several women in white dresses, and on said table a metal device. It was very oddly shaped, with the multiple chambers being hinted at from its shape and valves covering the surface, but as far as Lapiutalnice knew, it might as well have been an empty box. Nothing about the strange mass of cylinders reminded him of anything he had ever encountered before. Glancing over to see his wife's reaction, he could tell she had no clue what was going on either, and probably hadn't deduced much more than him.

Seeing these blank expressions, the commander gestured to the device and said, "This is the empire's most grand achievement to date, though it will hopefully soon be replaced by yours."

"So this is the answer to our dilemma," the elf man whispered, knowing that the commander would not lie about this. He would not have brought them here based on theoretics; it was clear there was too much risk for that. This metal box, whatever it was, would solve their problems. Whatever it was it could create and sustain more energy than Nulaidutice's rubber coils.

"Indeed," one of the elf women whose tight blond bun was turning to white replied, walking over from the machine. Gesturing for the elf woman to step forward, she opened a hatch near the top to reveal a contained basin of sorts, clearly meant to hold liquid, though it was dry now. "We engineers back in Tivowichaisch have been toying with the concept for a century while trying to amplify pitch's explosive qualities to relieve the empire's dependence on gunpowder. Unfortunately, no progress was made on that front, at least none that could out-compete Dark Elf production, but instead we got this. They call it the petrol engine, and this device will change everything. It takes refined pitch, called petrol, trapping it in the engine and combusting it. This creates vast amounts of energy trapped inside to be released by the motor, more than we've ever thought we'd achieve. Many things that were impossible are now possible. Boats that can go upstream, vehicles that can pull great weight, and even..."

"Machines that can fly," Nulaidutice finished quietly as she looked down in wonder. The imperial engineer nodded her head, and then went quiet to allow the Fienlapus to process what they had just heard. Though his wife seemed to inspect the device a bit further, he knew she was too awestruck to really let any of it in. She had been looking for this solution for the better part of a week, and now it had simply been granted to them as if by Lady Luck herself. She had every right to have no further comment, and after awhile dropped the guise of studying the machine alltogether.

When the two elves only stood there dumbfounded for a what felt like an eternity, the commander finally spoke again, "I don't think I need to tell you your duty in this. You two will go down in history as the inventor of the first airborne vessel and the first elf to fly, and of course you will be reimbursed for your efforts. Your ladyship will be offered a position among these fine women as the first aeronautical engineer, and your husband the position of first pilot. I speak these things on behalf of our empress, who will be meeting with you before the week is out." When the two elves simply stood there, leaning on each other for support the commander sighed and signaled for the guards to open the door. "After we get a splint on that leg you may go home tonight to pack your belongings, we will set down the road to Tivowichaisch and the City of a Thousand Trees tomorrow morning." Then silently the two were inspected, and rode straight back to their homestead once the elf man's injuries were tended to.

It had been growing dark while they rode, and night when they arrived. There was no crowd, which surprised Lapiutalnice, until he spotted a soldier patrol off in the distance. They had formed a perimeter around their house, for they did not want the mob disturbing them or learning what they had been told. Until they were under the watchful gaze of the empress herself the commander wasn't going to take risks. Simultaneously Lapiutalnice was glad not to deal with the mess and dreading what was to come. He had achieved his dream, and as he feared it was slowly turning into a nightmare.

His wife seemed to think the same thing, for as soon as they were allowed into the privacy of their own home she turned and hugged her husband fiercely. "Well, at least the empress appreciates your efforts, Lapiu." Her muffled voice was shaky, though she was not crying yet. Her husband was at this point, however, finally able to breathe and let his emotions out in private.

"At least it isn't all bad," he tried to assure himself, stroking the very hair he was soaking with his tears. "Though clenched in Failatgie's fist, you'll finally be recognized for your skills, Nulai. I always said you were wasted out here." He could feel her tensing up at the remark, getting ready to reject his rationality, until out of the darkness came a whistle that made them both jump.

Grasping for the sword he kept by the door, the elf man was in a panic to defend himself and his wife from the invaders that were already onto them, but he was cut short when the voice continued in a whisper, "Calm down, it's me, Piqoug! I've been hiding out here since the crash, down in your cellar once the soldiers started crowd control. They haven't let up the patrols since, and these aren't all frontier soldiers, some of these are imperial guard from Paipadaívaen. You've got attention from the City of a Thousand Trees, which isn't surprising in itself, but the empress must really want you guys quiet if she is trapping you so fast."

"We were shown something top secret good friend," Nulaidutice sighed in relief, moving to light a lamp until the bird man grabbed her arm and shook his head. "That's a good point, especially having talked to a harpy right afterwards they'll assume we told you. They'll hunt you down for the rest of your days if they catch you here."

"I can fly," the shadow of a bird whispered. "Until they build your machine, they won't be able to catch me. I'll just move to a new aerie associated with human empires. You two honestly are the only reason I haven't already. The real question is what are you two going to do?"

In the darkness it was almost impossible to tell, but the elf couple exchanged a look of despair. Though Piqoug could not see it, he could read the silence and whispered, "I was only half-joking about Muyítselt'e. They are a part of Trulpanun, but that empire is far too busy trying to keep itself together to worry about a few elves moving within its borders. You could disappear into one of those mountain villages and no one would be the wiser."

"And how do you propose we escape our current situation?" Nulaidutice stated a little more icily than intended, but this merely earned her a birdlike smirk even she could have read if it wasn't pitch black.

"Your Lapudrum hasn't been standardized yet; people never look up."

The Epilogue

Leaving the steamy cloud forests behind, the elf commander wiped the sweat from his brow once again. His blue uniform was coated in mud, his weary squad covered in bug bites and sunburns – the pale-skinned soldiers followed their guide to a remote village high up in the mountains. Just past the last trees in the mist, the dark-skinned human stood waiting with an amused look on his face, watching the elves struggle through his homeland. Once they reached him, a hand emerged from his richly decorated red poncho, causing the tassels all over it to sway as it did, pointing toward the collection of bamboo and hardwood structures built along the steep slope.

The village was ancient according to the guide, but to the elf commander it looked like it was about to slide off the mountainside, more built into it the cliff than on top of the bluff. Maybe it was ancient in human terms, he thought to himself; only they were insane enough to live in a place like this until it inevitably slid off. Of course, he had to correct himself, there were two elves out there insane enough they might try.

Thanking his guide in choppy Danpunal, he and his squadron began their march up the narrow ledge toward the winding streets, if that is what they could be called. The whole place gave him vertigo, and he kept to the rock wall as much as he could, letting the amused-looking humans and splotchy ningyo pass on the cliff side. Looking around he saw what he expected: human men and women in colorful sashes and robes moving about their business, bone and stone jewelry jingling as they did. Clusters of the diminutive koi men could also be seen wandering the mountainside, their scales a patchy mess of oranges and blacks and fins weighed down with piercings. He had gotten used to their presence in this region by now – the ningyo had lived with their human companions here for as long as the humans could remember, even if the elves knew a time when they didn't.

The amount of harpies was certainly different, though. The bird folk could be seen talking at the merchant huts, bartering for the chocolate and fruits they gathered and grew in the thick rainforest below. But he knew there was a red-feather aerie nearby, and that likely explained the heavy air traffic beyond the free fall on his left. To the red harpies – and even a familiar black one he thought he spotted soaring on the intense updraft with ease – this was the perfect place for flying. He understood now why his targets might be drawn to a place like this.

Because for all the diversity he had seen thus far, there was one more race he was hoping to find, and thus he started asking around, did anyone in this village know an elf couple? Much to his shock, the first two ningyo he addressed responded nonchalantly, "Do you mean the Feenlapu? They live further up into the pass, you know them?" With this the elderly fish men with whiskers so long they drooped down to their laps turned their bulbous eyes toward the squad, looking suspiciously at the foreign soldiers from under their large brows.

"They are wanted back in Failatgie for high treason and desertion," the elf man said stiffly, though inwardly he was just satisfied with being so close to finishing his hunt. He had only been in Trulpanun for a couple months, but it was draining. Almost as bad as that time he led a skirmish in the southern islands of Teulyakeo, but at least then he had elvish accommodations – even the Golothi were so far behind them that he struggled to stay in human lands long. At least there the weather wasn't oppressive.

His accusation, once again to his surprise, was met by a croaking chuckle from one of the fish men, "That explains a lot about them. We all wondered why they were so excited to move to some backwater chocolate town. We just thought it was because of the wind."

"The wind?" the elf commander responded with intense confusion. He had thought the humans were bad, but the ningyo might be taking the cake for most oblivious people he had ever spoken to. "What do you mean the wind?"

"Look behind you, I think your old pals might have been tipped off. The traitors seem to have known you were here! But unless you can sprout wings yourself I think you're going to have trouble reaching them!" cackled the other fish man, nearly knocking down the wooden game pieces as he did. To this the elves all whipped around to watch as a strange device came soaring past the ledge. He recognized it immediately, though it was not powered this time. The strong updraft was more than enough to carry the Lapudrum through the air as it soared away from danger.

Inside the craft he could make out the wild blonde hair of his target, and the deep brown of her husband's. However, perched at the back of the machine just behind the tail, he saw a tiny pale face looking back at him, their wild brown hair whipping in the wind as they sailed over the trees, banking to continue following the mountainside off toward where he presumed the aerie would be. Far out of his reach unless he wanted to make the long climb to the top of a mountain.

One of his men began to raise his gun, pointing the rifle to try his best at making a shot, though the target was moving fast. Shaking his head, the commander gently lowered the barrel, much to the elf's surprise. "I can make the shot, sir, you know we've been trained to hit harder."

"It's over, soldier," the commander said, the hint of a smile hanging at the edge of his face, "Let's not start an international crisis this far from home. It took us a month to track them down, and agents from Teulyakeo probably don't even know to look. They're hiding, not plotting, we'd probably be creating more danger chasing them than just leaving them alone. It's time to head home."

"And tell the empress what?" the soldier replied in shock. "That we marched through the jungle for a month only to let deserters with valuable war information escape?"

"No," he replied, gazing off into the clouds where the machine was now banking upwards, coasting on its momentum up the mountain slopes toward the aerie. "We'll tell her the truth. They are far beyond the practical reach of harm and our ability to catch now. They might as well have vanished from the earth. We can simply say, 'They were swallowed up by the sky.'"

Appendix

Beastfolk: (Old Elvish: *Mûlnprês* /məlnprɛs/)

A catchall term for the many races that possess both the features of the elder races (such as bipedality and sentience) and the features of various animal groups. Though many of them have been around in the world for millennia, only the four elder races have been around for all of recorded history (as recorded by the elves at least, the memories of humans and dwarves being much shorter). Though forgotten by some, the elves not only remember a time without them but know they are responsible for their existence. Many of the beastfolk were created by the elves to overcome their own physical limitations before their military technology was unrivaled. It is a bitter point for them that no race they have created have they succeeded in controlling, the creation of life proving far easier than managing it. Thus the beastfolk have slipped into the rest of the world, either creating space or claiming the regions the elder races had left vacant. Some are well-established parts of the global society, while others are isolated in the remote corners of the world. Their attitudes and the role they play are as diverse as the animals they bear in their blood.

Brödbrutal: (Dwarvish: *Brödbrutal* /ˌbrudb̥rəˈt̥al/)

The central plateau and mountain chain are vast and known by many names. The southeastern branch of smooth, weathered sandstone is known as the Brödbrutal by its main inhabitants, the diminutive Peks. Peks, though most populous with formal warring city-states and deep-reaching mines, are far from the only inhabitants of these mountains, with both clans of orcs and the beastfolk clans wandering nomadically through these dry hills.

Brutally hot by day, with bone-chilling winds smoothing out the peaks by night, it is a hostile environment that is lucrative in mineral wealth. It is especially known for its geode and coal deposits as well as vast quantities of pitch bubbling up from the mysterious depths of the world.

City of a Thousand Trees: (West Elvish: *Noírailaitoisanal* /ŋoiɹailait̪ˌoiʂanˈal/)

A common title for the city of Paipadaívaen, given for its sheer size. Among the most populous cities of elves in the world, Paipadaívaen spans a large section of woodland, a network of platforms, buildings, and bridges all hung between the awe-inspiring silver maples for which Tivowichaisch is famous. Even on the forest floor, vast stretches of parkland and roads for transporting bulk goods tame the wilderness with civilization. Thus visitors to the beating heart of Western Elf civilization coined the title for the grand city, and it actually sees more use outside Paipadaívaen than within.

Dacitcué: (West Elvish: *Dácitcué* /d̪aˈkʔiut͡s/)

The name of an inland sea in Haentailg, though it is often referred to as "the lake" by locals. Despite this name, Dacitcué is far too wide to see across and more than big enough to allow for water traffic in the summer months, when the lake is not frozen over. The river, which feeds into this large body of water, is one of the major trade routes out of the Brödbrutals for Pekish merchants coming down from the mountains to trade with Failatgie. This was a dangerous trade route due to the threat of orcish raids out on the steppe. However, with the establishment of Gaités up the river, it has become one of the main sources of material goods for the Western Elvish Empire. Still, due to the harsh climate, the lake remains a backwater territory, like the rest of Haentailg. A crossroad between the much more populous woodlands and the Petty Pek Kingdoms up in the hills.

Daechûg: (West Elvish: *Daechûg* /deˈt͡ʃeəg/)

The name for the transitional lands between the forests of Tivowichaisch and the Haentailg steppelands. These grasslands have a bloody history, being contested between the nomadic orc clans and the Western Elves, who once dwelt in the Daechûg before being pushed from the mainland entirely thousands of years ago. Though the orcs don't remember this, and as far as they're concerned the steppes are their ancestral homeland, the elves have a very long memory and began to take back what they feel was taken from them. It took hundreds of years and the adoption of gunpowder to gain a foothold, for the orcs, being stronger and faster than elves, held the advantage in open land. Yet the elves eventually retook the fertile plains both for farming and as a buffer between orcish raids and the imperial heartland in Tivowichaisch. With the invention of the Gaité system, the population of Plains Elves living out in the Daechûg was allowed to grow, managing farms and the forts along the frontier.

Danpunal: (Danpúnult Hág'e: *Danpúnal* /danˈpɯːnal/)

An ethnic and linguistic group of humans living on the southwestern peninsula, often known as the Children of the Djinn. Forming the bulk of the Trulpanun Empire, they dominate the human cultural sphere, with many of the major cities of the human world at least being under Trulpanun rule, if not ethnically Danpunal. Though there are many cultural groups among the Children of the Djinn, they share many cultural and physical features. These include the reverence of spirits referred to as the djinn (except the elephant worshipers of the far west), speaking a dialect of Danpúnult (some of which are distinct enough to be unintelligible), and large builds with dark skin, even for humans. They are also regularly stereotyped by outsiders with the color red, due to it being such a common dye color, especially among the desert-dwelling nomads. But they hold no association with it themselves, the color choice being more practical than conscious.

Dark Elves: (West Elvish: *Laígvâi* /ˈʟaigˌβaiə/)

Dark Elves, sometimes referred to as Mountain Elves due to them dwelling in the small mountainous regions on the borders of the two empires, are the only elves to not technically belong to either empire in their entirety. These exotic elves, with ebony-colored skin and blood-red eyes, live in grand, fabulously wealthy cave cities that self-rule for the most part. It is the production of gunpowder that allows for both this wealth and independence, the secrets of which are guarded jealously by the influential families that rule the mountain slopes. Constant infighting plagues the region, both from within and provoked as both empires try to dominate the gunpowder trade from outside, but to no avail. Warfare in the mountains is hard, and the foothold these war profiteers have proven hard to dislodge. Besides, the secret of gunpowder cannot be risked being eradicated either, for it is the line between survival and extinction for the elves. This leaves the Dark Elves with a strange sense of pious pride in their duty as stewards of their salvation, while simultaneously violent cartels and cabals known for ruthless tactics and a disregard for the social prudishness of other elves.

Dwarves: (Old Elvish: *Whad* /ʍad/)

Robust in both mind and body, dwarves are a stocky race, often dwelling in smaller-scale societies along the remote edges of the world. Physically strong for their size and notoriously stubborn, their perceived rigidity belies a fiercely independent and curious nature. This leads dwarves to first and foremost be a naturally creative race, known for the beauty of the things they make just as much as their crudeness and stubbornness. This makes them frustrating to the other elder races, for they are regularly pioneers in discovery and technological advancement, being able to see the world in ways the other races have closed their minds to. Yet they also mock their social norms and unspoken rules, invaluable to work with and insufferable to be around at the same time. Perhaps this is why dwarvish society rarely grows greater than a coalition of underground cities, and even what they call an empire is more of a loose confederation, but these judgments do not bother the dwarves. To them this is simply as the world should be, beholden to those you choose and your hands suffering no vision other than your own.

Elder Races: (Old Elvish: *Þâfprês* /θæɸprɛs/)

The elder races is a catchall term used in some scholarly circles to refer to the four oldest-known species of sentient creatures in the world. There is no record of the world that does not possess these races, and even as they were joined by younger races (usually the beastfolk, but there are exceptions) the four elder races have remained the most populous and dominant peoples of the world. Of these are the humans, populous social creatures who are quick both to friendship and offense; the elves, long-lived and logically minded above all else; the dwarves, a stocky and brash, free-spirited people; and the orcs, brutal and warlike goliaths living among the hinterlands.

Elves: (Old Elvish: *Va* /va/)

Logical and long in years, their minds calculating and memories long, the elves are the physically weakest of the elder races but make up for this in mental prowess. Elves are shorter on average and built like a twig with pale skin that renders sunlight even harsh to them. They can live for centuries, but their birth rates are far lower than the other races, making it difficult to bounce back from plague or conflict. While these shortcomings weigh heavily in their minds, their sharp intellect has worked for thousands of years to overcome these weaknesses, carefully constructing both machine and society to compensate for their physical vulnerability. Their decisions can appear cold and uncaring to outsiders, but to the elf they are thoroughly calculated. Being able to enact plans that take centuries and having data obsessively compiled from millennia of natural observation, no other race has a better understanding of the world and its workings. This gives them a strength to lean on that the other races do not have, ensuring not only that they survive but also that they thrive despite the odds being stacked against them.

Failatgie: (West Elvish: *Failatgie* /ˈɸailatˌgie/)

The name for the Western Elf Empire in their own tongue, whose rival is Teulyakeo in the east, splitting what was once a unified elven empire between the two of them. Dominated by High Elven culture and centered around the highland forests of Tivowichaisch, Failatgie (or simply the empire) has been in a two-fronted war for around two thousand years. Having been fighting the orcish nomads off the steppe since time immemorial, a cultural rift formed between the Eastern Elves cloistered on their archipelago and the mainland Western Elves, whose blood formed a barrier to annihilation. Many other factors went into the divide, but the result was a cold civil war and cultural drift that has been ongoing for thousands of years. The pressure created a militant empire focused on survival and the hope of one day re-unifying the elvish world to protect it from the rest of the world. Leading them to obsessively advance in military technology that, to all but their eastern rivals, feels sophisticated to the point of magic. Grand galleons dwarf the galleys of the human world, and lines of shields are no match for elvish guns. Paired with their long lives and a logical mind that has turned cold in the harshness of war, the elves of Failatgie come off as intimidating and mythical despite their diminutive build compared to the rest of the races, a reputation only thousands of years of grit can build.

Gaité: (West Elvish: *Gaité* /gaitˌ/)

Taking hundreds of years to slowly regain a foothold in Haentailg, the elves needed a system to keep orcish raids out of their lands and thus prevent them from pushing the elves back into the forests of Tivowichaisch. Thus the Gaité system was devised to control the border between the orc clans and elvish farmland, cementing elvish rule over the fertile Daechûg. Gaités are timber forts and cannon platforms, allowing for a secure structure where the elves can fire upon the orcs while being relatively safe from a counteroffensive. The real genius of the Gaité system, though, was not in their design, which is simply cheap and practical, but in their use. Spaced out at even intervals along the border where the fertile fields of the forest steppe transition turned into the poor soil of the steppe proper, no Gaité was out of eyesight from another. When properly staffed, there is no spot on the border the Western Elf Empire does not have eyes upon, and troops can be called from neighboring Gaités in case of raid or invasion. Small towns were established around each one, both to staff and feed the fort, making them relatively self-sustaining as long as powder and gear were supplied, leading to a simple yet effective system that cost little for as effective as it was.

Goloth: (Golahaag: *Goloth* /ˈɡolaθ/)

The remnants of an ancient human civilization, Goloth is what remains of a vast kingdom controlling the shores of the Kutgie Sea. Still one of the wealthiest and most advanced of the human regions, the old kingdom slowly fell to infighting among petty princes and the armies of Trulpanun until only a small city-state remained. Despite the rest of their civilization being conquered, the small valley kingdom of Goloth is not going to disappear anytime soon, as Trulpanun has tried to conquer the impenetrable city simply referred to as "The Throne" many times. Each of these attempts has been squashed with ease, for the Throne is a city of mythical proportions and has the highest population of any place on earth. The Children of the Law are also a proud and defiant people, whether in or outside the Throne. The religious influence Goloth has over its former territories has been proven easier for the southern empire to work with rather than suppress. Believing themselves to be the oldest civilization on earth and their sacred valley to be the birthplace of humanity, the Children of the Law remain stuck in the past. This is likely why their influence seems to be shrinking, despite their stubbornness to persist, as it refuses to adapt to the future.

Haentailg: (West Elvish: *Haentáilg* /henˌtaiəlɡ/)

Haentailg is the elvish name of the steppe between the woodlands of Tivowichaisch and the Brödbrutal mountain chain. It is populated by the Plains Elves, but their presence is predominantly in the Daechûg, where the forests transition into open grasslands, while orcish clans still roam the far-out parts of the steppe. The temperature is aggressively dry, swinging between intense heat in the summer and frigid snow in the harsh winters, with poor soil outside of the transition zone. The elves see no reason to push further into Haentailg, but the orcs thrive in the lands no one else wants. With huge herds of livestock, they take advantage of the empty seas of grass until they turn to scrubland and sandy deserts in the north.

Harpies: (Harpy: *Nongháqìeçi* /ɲoɴˌháˈqìeçi/)

One of the youngest races, their birth on the isle of Laetail half a millennium ago shook the world. Though birdlike in many of their features, with scaly, taloned hands and legs along with feathers covering most of their bodies, their minds are sharp and most definitely sentient. With wings that hang down from their arms like sleeves of feathers that can be flexed stiff and hollow bones that make the harpy deceptively light for their size, they possess an ability all other races had only dreamed of: the gift of flight. Overnight this changed the very fabric of society, and as the harpies flew to escape coercion by one group, they simply found themselves in the territory of another. Being born so late, the harpies could find no land to call their own; they had no choice but to bow to the demands of the elder races. Separating themselves from the rest as best they can in aeries far up in the mountains, they act as the best messengers and scouts the world has ever seen. Their global society acts as a delivery system faster than anything dreamed before it. It was in this that the harpies found their revenge as well, however, for there has never been a greater coalition of data brokers in the past either.

Being so widespread, harpies have grown into multiple ethnicities, though with only five hundred years of history and a large amount of genetic and cultural exchange, they have not distinguished themselves from each other too strongly yet. They are usually referred to by feather color (such as the Blackfeather Harpies of Laetail or the Redfeather Harpies of southern Trulpanun), but each aerie has its own distinguishing colors and patterns that the harpies themselves use to identify each other and where they come from. With so much pressure from outside of their race, harpies frequently band together despite what little differences have formed rather than letting those drive them apart. United in bitterness towards the world outside of the aeries and a desire to shirk it once the moment presents itself. These hopes manifested in a mythical group almost all harpies share some belief in. A people who have established a floating city far above the world, a city to which their race can flee out of the reach of their enemies. Alas, such a city must not exist, or else why have the harpies not simply flown away? The answers vary by religious group and region, but the simplest answer is, sadly, that no such city likely exists.

High Elves: (West Elvish: *Maiyivâi* /ˈmaiˌjiβaiə/)

Proud elves hailing from Tivowichaish, the vast forests at the center of the Failatgie Empire, the High Elves are one of the most powerful and influential groups of elves in the world. Building grand cities in the groves of monolithic silver maples, their large population and robust economy allowed them to dominate the Western Elvish regions. Their fierce tenacity and advanced educational system are the two factors that have allowed the High Elves to achieve the most advanced military technology to date, their only rivals being the Teulyakeo Empire to the east. But the Eastern Elves lack the military-minded mentality of their western sisters, especially within the High Elves. A mentality that has led to an obsession with the space where elegance meets practicality, creating a reputation of a semi-mythical grace to the other elves they lord over. Beautiful and efficient, the true embodiment of what it means to be a Western Elf.

Humans: (Old Elvish: *Han* /han/)

Humanity is the strangest of the four elder races, for physically and intellectually they are the most average. They are not renowned for great works like the dwarves, known for being as learned as the elves, nor do they have the strength of orcs. Yet humanity dominates an entire hemisphere of the world, for the human superpower does not lie in the individual but in the collective. Humans are emotional and social creatures, forming strong ties in shared experiences. This has led to them establishing many strong nations with huge populations. The ability to rally humans around a cause is legendary, but so is their tendency to abandon them. While having the potential for an amount of empathy that confuses the other races, humans are most known for their flighty nature and ability to be swayed by charismatic influence. Yet their ability to build and maintain such large political structures, regardless of their stability, has led to them being a looming presence in the world. They are a center of trade and power whether the other races wish to put up with their antics or not.

Island Elves: (East Elvish: *Lak Vei Tashi* /lak βei taˈʃi/)

A sister group to the Sea Elves, the Island Elves dwell on the vast archipelago in the eastern sea. Once the refuge of the elves as they fled orcish invasions, it has remained one of the most populous regions of elves to the modern day. The weather of these islands, fueled by the cold water coming in from the north, is surprisingly dry and unpredictable. Whole regions will swing from dry land to monsoonal marshes throughout the year, but in the long lives of elves, these changes feel frequent and familiar. Instead of relying on the unpredictable and ever-changing shores they live on, their culture has turned to the rich bounty of the seas that surround them. The seaways of the archipelago are some of the richest on earth, the place where the cold northern waters and the southern seas meet, with huge schools of fish that the Island Elves quickly adapted to take advantage of. To this day Island Elf ships are the fastest and most prized in the world, even if they do not have the capacity of their Sea Elf cousins. This has prevented the Western Elves from gaining a foothold in those islands despite dominating the open sea.

Laetail: (West Elvish: *Laetail* /leˈtail/)

A large island located centrally in the Nalchraihaniel Sea, it is probably one of the most important regions in the elvish world outside the Dark Elf city-states. The mainland north of Laetail is occupied by orcish clans living in a hostile land. Marching through steppe, desert, and swamp to cross from the elvish world to the domain of humanity would be a treacherous journey. So merchants take advantage of the sea instead, which means taking advantage of Laetail. The island is a midway point on this journey and allows elvish merchants a chance to rest in its mild, sunny climate on the way home with goods produced in the human lands out west. Despite the hostility the two elvish empires hold toward each other, a truce has been formed on this island to allow merchants from both empires to utilize its ports (allowing them to focus their fighting over militarily strategic locations rather than economical ones). On top of this increased diversity, Laetail is also the birthplace of the harpies and home of the Blackfeather Harpy Aerie, the largest in the world. Thus, while a wealthy territory with some degree of self-rule, the island is also a mess of competing interests and claims, leading to a bubbling unrest beneath the surface constantly threatening to well up.

Lapiutalnice: (West Elvish: *Lapiutalnicé* /laˈpiutalnˌies/)

A Sea Elvish man living who was transferred to the town of Natniln during his service time as a soldier. He was moved there to reinforce the Gaité system along the orcish frontier, a highly sensitive region to the Western Elvish Empire that has not seen real conflict in decades. Though possessing some family in the area (who had been moved in earlier years for similar reasons), Lapiutalnice is far closer to his wife, Nulaidutice, whom he had met out on the frontier. He also has a friend in Piqoug, a harpy courier he met while working the Gaités. He would spend breaks with the bird man to hear his stories of the wider world to avoid feeling trapped out at the edge of the steppe.

Lapudrum: (Old Elvish: *Lapudrum* /lapudrum/)

The name Lapiutalnice gave to the flying machine he was creating, meaning sky boat. Its name is derived from the Old Elvish language, the predecessor to the modern languages and still utilized as a language of learning in many corners of the world. Ancient texts are often written in it, and access to these ancient records, in which the early elves cataloged the movements of the stars, waves, and winds, is essential for doing research and science. Thus, for consistency, records and technological terms are still named in the old tongue, while commentaries and speech are done in the modern elvish languages.

Muyitselt'e: (Danpúnult Hág'e: *Muyítselt'e* /mə'jiːt͡sel̩t?e/)

The most eastern of the Danpunal regions, Muyitselt'e is a series of tropical mountain provinces under the rule of the Trulpanun Empire. They border the Nalchraihaniel Sea in the west and are one of the main stops for elvish merchants on the way to the rest of the human world. The region is the main producer of chocolate in the world, which is a cash crop that dries and ships well, making those who live in the region some of the richest on earth. They also produce large quantities of coffee, which the elves covet and exchange for the tobacco humanity craves. Despite the lush, cloudy forests climbing onto the steep slopes being where their crops are grown, most of the population does not live in these dark, humid woodlands. The villages of the Muyitselt'e are built along the cloud line, just above where the billowing clouds from the sea try and fail to crest the peaks, dumping their moisture upon the soaked forests below (their residents referred to as the Children of the Clouds). Built on top of plateaus or even into the mountain slopes themselves, they suspend themselves above the swarming insects and diseases of the jungle, with their most populous cities lying farther into the mountains among terraced farmland. Cities they share with the Riverfolk, a race of diminutive fish people who have been living among their human neighbors so long they have formed a mixed-race society. Something the rest of the empire finds unsettling, but considering their wealth, they put up with this strange arrangement to keep the peace.

Nalchraihaniel: (West Elvish: *Nálchraihaeniel* /ŋalˌʃɹaiˈheniel/)

The gulf between the elvish and human worlds, Nalchraihaniel is a sea bordered in the east by the Sea Elven lands and the Children of the Clouds living in Muyitselt'e in the west. The vast steppes and swamps inhabited by orcish clans make the northern shore of the sea difficult for either the elves or humans to get a foothold on, making overland routes between the two worlds dangerous. But orcs rarely venture into the churning chaos of the ocean, and thus, where no highway exists overland, Nalchraihaniel became a network of trade between the human and elvish empires. Grand Sea Elf merchant ships from one of the many trading companies make the trips back and forth, exporting cotton, spices, and tea in exchange for rubber and spices native to the human world (with chocolate and coffee being highly sought after). The island of Laetail historically was a base of operations for these trading missions. Being centrally located in the northern part of Nalchraihaniel and not connected to the mainland, Laetail has been an ideal stop for ships to rest at on their way back from the human lands. While Failatgie technically owns the island, a treaty dictates ports must be open to Eastern Elvish merchant ships too, leading to the waters of Nalchraihaniel being diverse in the merchants who tread the watery road between elvendom and humanity.

Natniln: (West Elvish: *Nátniln* /ŋatˈniln/)

A Gaité town in Daechûg, its small population exists to man the fort sitting at the edge of the steppe. Outside military work to help keep the fort up and running, the town's main occupation is the growing of oats and sunflowers. There are some livestock, but large herds were dubbed as too much of a target for orcish raids (who aren't concerned about the cereal crops), and thus livestock farms are kept to a minimum, with most meat being purchased from neighboring towns. Being a Gaité town, it has little to no export and a culture more similar to a military camp than a rural village, but all these sacrifices are made up for in the prestige that comes with serving on the front lines in the millennia-old war against the orcs.

Ningyo: (Ningyo: *Hikháph Ònokhí* /hiˈχœːpʼ ˈɤˌnoχyː/)

Among the oldest of the beastfolk races, one that only the elves remember a time in the world without, the ningyo are a group of fish folk sharing many characteristics with domestic koi. With colorful, scaly skin, bulbous foreheads, and large, bubble-like eyes, the ningyo are relatively short on average and just as happy in the water as they are outside of it. With gills along the sides of their ribcage that they can pump water to instead of their lungs and delicate-looking fins on their legs and arms, they are surprisingly agile swimmers. They mostly live in the shadows of human civilizations, even living among them in the Muyitselt'e region of the Trulpanun empire, though their relations with humans aren't usually so cooperative. Often they live up in the regions abandoned by humans due to a great conflict that rendered the region too haunted to rebuild. But the ningyo learned how to coexist with these ghosts just as they learned how to coexist with people of Muyitselt'e, their social adaptability proving as versatile as their ability to dwell in water and land.

Nulaidutice: (West Elvish: *Núláiduticé* /ɳuˌlaiəˈduties/)

A fierce Wood Elvish woman who developed a stubborn attitude to survive her college career. Looking to study engineering and escape the dismal bayou that the Wood Elves are native to, she went to college in Tivowichaisch, where she was immediately met with pushback. The elves of the central highlands have a habit of looking down upon those on the fringes of the Failatgie Empire, especially Wood Elves, who are considered stubborn and backwards. Ironically, the pressure to be taken seriously molded Nulaidutice into as much of a stereotypical Wood Elf as one can be, and she graduated with good honors despite the prejudice. Taking the most reputable position that took her farthest from Tivowichaisch, she headed out to the Gaité town of Natniln after her two decades of education were finished. While using her degree to work on making and maintaining forts along the frontier, she met her husband, Lapiutalnice, at the Gaité. He was an odd choice of husband to her coworkers and friends, who took her far more seriously outside of Tivowichaisch. But she seemed to see something in the lazy man caught more often trying to fly a kite than doing his duties. Since her own work ethic never laxed nobody questioned things too strongly, allowing the couple to marry without fueling the rumor mill too greatly.

Orcs: (Old Elvish: *Nûd* /nəd/)

Among the four elder races, orcs are by far the strongest and most physically fit of their kin. Towering over humans and elves, let alone dwarves, and built proportionally more muscular than others, orcs have a ferocious and violent reputation. Forming warrior clans moving with their vast herds of animals in the harsh parts of the world, the orcs strike out upon the other three in raids on their borderlands. Orcs can attack out of nowhere and disappear back to nowhere before a response can be made, proving a constant threat for as long as anyone can remember. To the orcs, might does not make right but simply is right, the proclaimed will of Death, whom they worship as a god. Though far less populous due to their environment and tendency for infighting, a single orc warrior is worth several soldiers of any other race in both strength and skill. Thus renowned for not only their warlike nature and violence but also having the skills to back up and exceed those expectations, the rest of the world fears the orcs as dangerous barbarians more so than any other race.

Paipadaívaen: (West Elvish: *Paipadaívaen* /ˌpʔaipaˈɖaiven/)

The capital city of Failatgie and seat of the imperial senate and the crown. It has long been the seat of Western Elf power, being centrally located in the highland forests of Tivowichaisch, allowing for the High Elves of the region to both exert military and logistical influence over their neighbors. Having been fighting a two-fronted war for almost two thousand years, Paipadaívaen and the empress who dwells there hold the West Elvish lands in a firm grip, leading to mixed feelings from the city's subjects. But the elvish nature is logical, so the city is allowed to centralize the wealth of the empire in exchange for protection. For the advancement of Paipadaívaen is the advancement of the empire, something the frontier elves know they will not survive without the protection of.

Pek: (Dwarvish: *Pæk* /pɛk/)

Living in their dense city-states atop the mesas of the Bröd-brutals, the Opal Dwarves, more commonly known as Peks, are a peculiar breed. Though short and artistic like their dwarven cousins, their pointed ears and beardless faces seem almost elvish in nature, and their mindset is completely alien to both. They're fiercely independent and engineeringly minded, which has led to them being known as the powder keg region by their neighbors. Many innovations in gunpowder technology have been used by them to bring competing city-states off their mountaintops. The region is in perpetual conflict fueled by elvish gunpowder in exchange for the metals they mine. Though cute-looking to many outsiders, one should not underestimate their tenacity and cruel, calculating efficiency, but that is not all there is to them. Also known for their textiles and dye trading, the Peks are recognized for their elegance as well as their ruthlessness.

Piqoug: (Harpy: *Píqoùg* /ˈpʲíqoùɢ/)

A Blackfeather Harpy courier from the isle of Laetail. Being from such a large aerie so centrally located between the human and elvish worlds, the young harpy was given the unique opportunity to interact with both cultures extensively. Even occasionally making it to the petty Pek kingdoms north of the elvish empires. While it is far more typical for harpies to be more aloof and businesslike, not particularly eager to get friendly with the other races, Piqoug could not handle the long flights between Laetail and the far-reaching regions it delivered to. Thus he began making drinking buddies along his routes to relieve the monotony. Though he had far more success in the human region of Muyitselt'e, he did manage to make friends with an elf soldier named Lapiutalnice in the small town of Natniln along the orcish frontier.

Plains Elves: (West Elvish: *Îpvâi* /iəpˈβaiə/)

One of the youngest groups of elves, the Plains Elves split from the other Western Elves as they colonized the recently captured steppe from the orcs, which Failatige continually pushes further inland. Yet, they have already formed a distinct identity for themselves as a border people, being practical and stern before all else. The forest-steppe transition is a very fertile region, causing them to be an agricultural powerhouse, leading in the production of most cereals in the world. Their lives revolve around the farm and the vast stretch of border they live on, many living in the constant shadows of the border forts known as Gaités. Even when one of these forts is not physically nearby, their presence is felt in the almost military-esque way they run their towns and farms. There is little time for fun out on the plains; survival takes up all the community's energy when sharing a border with their oldest and most feared enemy.

Sea Elves: (West Elvish: *Nikvâi* /nikˈβaiə/)

The westernmost group of elves, still living along the shore of the sea on which they came to their land, the Sea Elves are probably the most important group of elves to the Failatige Empire, whether the High Elves will admit it or not. Living in well-fortified stone cities on the coast, their proximity to the sea has led to them becoming master shipwrights, only rivaled by their Island Elf cousins in the east. While those elves focus more on faster and smaller ships for short-trip transport of goods from island to island, the Sea Elves are known for the great ocean-going galleons that facilitate trade between the elves and the world of humans, as well as give their empire the edge in open waters. Being well traveled, the face of the Sea Elf is what humanity has come to associate with the elven race as a whole and gifted the Sea Elves with a broader perspective than their kin. A perspective that sometimes gets them in trouble with their High Elf neighbors.

Teulyakeo: (East Elvish: *Teulyakiō* /ˌteəˌlaˈkeu/)

Teulyakeo is the other half of the once unified elvish empire, holding dominion over the vast archipelago while their western cousins in Failatgie hold much of the mainland elvish territories. Unlike the Western Elves, the Eastern Elves are less militant and much more culturally diverse, being more of a confederation of many elvish ethnicities formed as a front against the Western Elves rather than a cohesive empire. However, the focus on learning, art, and wisdom should not fool outsiders into thinking unity is not a concern to the Eastern Elves, and as the High Elves dominate the west, the elves of the grand island, Niss Geō Sheweni, keep the confederation together in the east and long for a reunification of the ancient elvish empire as well. Though earning their place of respect through their House of Wisdom in their capital, Teuthek va ōn Geō, rather than through military logistics as their rival city of Paipadaívaen, it does not change the fact that the island of Niss Geō Sheweni uses its neighbors as military buffers in the same way the High Elves do.

Tivowichaisch: (West Elvish: *Zívowichaísch* /t͡si̜ˌβowiˈt͡ʃaiʃ/)

The highland forest region at the heart of the Failatgie Empire. It is the homeland of the High Elves, famous for its beautiful autumns, harsh winters, humid summers, and the grand silver maple trees that dominate the rolling hills of the region. Though the forests are stereotyped by the rest of the empire as privileged and populous, the reality is that this stereotype only really applies to the grand cities like Paipadaívaen and other university or military towns. Beyond the bustling treetop cities are countless hidden villages and homesteads eking out a living, lost in the surprisingly treacherous hills beyond the imperial highways connecting the forest to the rest of the world. These forgotten High Elves live their lives in the shadow of much grander powers, benefiting from the protection they afford to disappear from the prying eyes of their peers. More than elves live in those hills too, just out of sight, giving travelers pause before leaving the path in the woods.

Trulpanun: (Danpúnult Hág'e: *Trulpanún* /ˈtrəlpanˌɯːn/)

A human empire that rules the southwestern peninsula and most of the former Golothi Empire as well, meaning it holds dominion over most of humanity. As can be expected, this makes the empire fabulously wealthy, with the capital city of Opripakíl being a wonder of the world, built with ornate domes and thick walls to repel invaders that it has not had in a thousand years. But even far from the seat of the emperor in the distant south lie splendid cities among the jungles and mountains, rich off the coffee and chocolate trade. Though having a strong sense of both military and domestic engineering works like mills, aqueducts, and metallurgy, the technology of humanity pales in comparison to that of the elvish empires, with gunpowder especially being zealously guarded against making its way into the human nations. Trulpanun is also far less stable than either of the elvish empires, despite its opulence, and is far more frequently focused on keeping the conquered princes fighting each other and not rebelling against the imperial throne. Trulpanun is a vast tract of rugged land covering a diverse group of peoples, not all of whom are even human, and exploiting older grudges than the empire is really the only way to keep their eyes off their conqueror. But even despite this, the empire should not be underestimated, for most of the world's population lives inside its borders. They may not have the best technology nor the stability, but they outnumber their rivals ten to one, and the emperor's gluttony for expansion knows no bounds.

Wood Elves: (West Elvish: *Vlannvâi* /ˌβlaɳˈβaiə/)

In the pine forests and great cypress bayou in the east of Failatgie live the Wood Elves, who are the continental elves who have dwelt there the longest. Even when the orcs pushed the elves from the mainland, the Wood Elves were able to remain in their elevated cities above the swamps, which the orcs coming off the steppe were not eager to dwell in, and have maintained their identity as survivors ever since. With a reputation for being troublemakers and having a strong self-identity, Wood Elves are the most sidelined of the Western Elves and probably would be entirely irrelevant if not for their cash crops of cotton and tobacco. A fate most Wood Elves would find preferable: remaining with their "Marsh Man" and being left alone by the ambitious empire that rules them.

About the Author...

At the age of six years old, living in Whatcom County in Washington State, just shy of the Canadian border, Gabriel Huffman was sat down by his father and read "The Hobbit" by J.R.R. Tolkien. That small event kick-started his lifelong interest in writing fantasy and how the genre could be used beyond its typical bounds. Twenty years and a computer science degree from Western Washington University later, he had all the tools and willpower necessary to finally publish his first short story: "To Face a Lion". Though writing is his main form of art, he truly just loves being immersed in the joy and wonder of making things and hopes he was able to share a little bit of that joy with you.